Praise for Suzanne Proulx
and *Bad Blood*

"Proulx offers readers a delightful dose of death in this novel of hospital suspense. I thoroughly enjoyed it!"
—TESS GERRITSEN

"*Bad Blood* brings hospital politics and intrigue to life in a murder epidemic. Suzanne Proulx's smart sleuth, Victoria Lucci, is a ravishing risk manager in a life and death setting with many of its own rules. Fans of hospital drama will like this one."
—*Mystery Scene*

"[Vicky Lucci's] sarcastic but surprisingly warmhearted zest carries the reader through. . . . A funny, fast-paced read."
—*Publishers Weekly*

"Irresistible . . . The plots and subplots are intriguing and the pace never flags."
—*Romantic Times*

BAD MEDICINE

Suzanne Proulx

FAWCETT BOOKS • NEW YORK

ACKNOWLEDGMENTS

Being a writer is supposed to be a lonely job, but somehow I ended up with a large group of people who have contributed in many ways during the writing of this book. My guys—Vic, Marcel, Dylan, and Sam—kept me from feeling lonely. Many people provided much-appreciated support, encouragement, insider information on hostage negotiations, and wedding disaster stories, but are too modest (I hope that's it) to want their names mentioned. Deepest appreciation to Gwen Shuster-Haynes and Janene McCrillis for reading the whole manuscript, quickly, and providing very astute comments. All mistakes are, of course, the author's, but thanks to Janice Ford, who kept me from making an embarrassing goof in the naming of one of the main characters, and to Chris Goff, Dave Jones, Bob Strange, Diane West, and Louise Woodwar, all of whose suggestions improved the manuscript. Thanks to Nancy Yost and Shauna Summers for guidance and support. For inspiration, encouragement, and intangibles, thanks to Sandy Rubin, Karen Zajac, and Anita Culligan. And thanks to Neil Ayervais for introducing me to the Last Word.

BAD MEDICINE

1

I may be old-fashioned, but it seems to me you don't talk about wedding disasters at somebody's rehearsal dinner. But then, it isn't my party. The conversation I started dealt with ugly bridesmaid dresses, of which I have many. I don't know why Kate asked me what I was going to do to ruin her wedding.

Kate knows all my bad-wedding stories. For each garish gown, an anecdote. At my friend Rona's reception (pink satin with marabou trim), a late spring snowstorm collapsed the tent. During my brother Charlie's processional (Scarlett O'Hara in red-and-white checked taffeta, over a crinoline), a bridesmaid's oversprayed hair got too close to the flame of the candle she was carrying. At my friend Sylvia's (pale blue, puffed sleeve on the right, no sleeve and off-the-shoulder on the left), a groomsman unwittingly trod on the hem of the maid of honor's not terribly well-made dress, tearing it asunder at the waist and revealing— well, you can guess. A good deal more than a garter. My brother Bob (apricot, with lime green, aqua, and pink floral patterns) said, "I, Robert, take thee. . . ." and there was a *looong* silence before he came up with the bride's name. Compounding this error, he finished

Las Vegas, the stock market, various racetracks, you name it and her daddy has made money at it. We got back to Denver just in time, and just sober enough, for the walk-through at St. John's, after spending two days and two fun-filled nights in Las Vegas. We saw shows, we gambled, we saw stars, we ate, we drank, we shopped. Kate's father passed out poker chips like they were made of plastic—which they are, of course. When I cashed mine in I had $630, which is a lot more plastic than I expected after having lost at almost everything. I promptly turned my windfall into paper and blew most of it on shoes.

Our bridal dresses are Halstons in grownup colors, mauve for the bridesmaids, a subdued forest green for me, and Kate paid for them. I do know that, unlike every other wedding-party dress I've ever worn, I could wear this one again. To, for instance, the Academy Awards, should I be invited to attend.

"I'd just like to get to one wedding," says Kate's friend Sassy, who's sitting next to me and jiggling everything. I don't mean this in a bad way. What I mean is she's tapping her fingers on the table, shaking her foot, twitching in her chair, and in general acting like either something's sticking her somewhere or the male stripper she ordered is late.

Kate orders another bottle of champagne—actually we have been drinking it by the jeroboam, a new word in my vocabulary and one I heartily embrace.

"Looks like we're going to make a night of it. Again," Laura observes. Laura's the most subdued member of the group, a lawyer at the same firm where my friend Melinda works. I don't know how she got the

have helped. Like the one reflecting Kate's luminous glow.

I could be envious, or I could figure that, if it happened to Kate, it could happen to me. But the fact is, no one's even asked me to get married in ten years. My latest sweetie was making noises about moving in together. There I was thinking he was going to pop the question and wondering how to get out of it, and it turned out he just wanted a roommate. Just as well. He once told me he knew, as soon as he met Kelly (his ex-wife) that he was going to marry her, because she was the first girl he'd ever met whom he *didn't* want to have sex with. I never heard anything so perverse in my life.

I drain my champagne glass and somebody fills it. This is a *nice* way to live, at least for a few days. I guess eventually it would get old. Sure it would.

I wonder if there's a reason it was all done so fast, but surely Kate would have told me. If it were the usual, traditional reason for a hurry-up wedding Kate wouldn't be drinking so much.

Sassy hands the wine steward a camera and asks him to take a picture of us toasting the bride. Smelling money—or maybe just because conviviality's contagious—he smilingly agrees. While he checks out the camera, Sassy hands tubes of lipstick to me, Hilary, and Laura, and orders us to refresh our smiles. Freshly lipsticked, we bare our teeth like professional models.

"To wretched excess," Hilary says, lifting her glass, "even if you *don't* only get married once." We all lift our glasses. Just as the camera flashes, somebody's cell phone rings. The obliging waiter squeezes off one more

Why would Harley call me, at this hour? I haven't been in the office all week. It's been refreshing.

"Risk manager? *Risk* manager?" Hilary says. "I didn't know it was something that could be *managed*. Particularly at a *hospital*."

Kate hoots.

I hear talking in the background but Harley's not answering me, or maybe what I hear is the echo of all the chatter in this room.

I hit the end button. Dammit, if Harley called me, it must be important. Or he could have just forgotten I'm off till Monday. Or he could have hit my cell phone number on his speed dial by mistake. Or the Environmental Services—that's hospital-speak for the cleaning people—could have. Or . . . something.

"It was Harley," I say to Kate. "My boss," I announce to the table at large. I will leave it to Kate to explain that, if my boss is calling at this hour, something has hit the fan.

"Order me some coffee, if you see the waiter," I say, and lurch for the ladies' lounge.

It's brighter here, but not a lot brighter. I dial Harley's number. The phone rings, and to me it sounds lonely, as if it's ringing in a deserted office, which is good. Just as I think it's going to voice mail, Harley picks up.

"Harley. What's happening?" I try to sound calm and sober. I watch two extremely thin young women apply their weight in makeup at the mirror. "What do you need?"

Does Harley thank me for dutifully returning his call while I'm on vacation? He does not. He utters a short

"Lookabaugh was here. Asking to speak to Dr. Hawthorne. Or you."

I draw my breath in sharply. "He's there now?"

"He might be. Anyway he *was*. Didn't I say that?"

"Is Dr. Hawthorne on tonight?"

"She is," Harley says. "She's the deck doctor on OB. That wasn't where he was, though. He turned up on the burn unit."

This news makes me several degrees more sober. The burn unit is where Labor & Delivery used to be, before we opened our new women's wing. And Dr. Cynthia Hawthorne was Mrs. Lookabaugh's doctor. I start digging in my purse for ibuprofen.

I tell myself that Cindy Hawthorne has the sense to stay away from Lookabaugh. Maybe he went away and won't come back. But Harley is still at the hospital, for some reason.

"I'm on my way." I wait for Harley to reassure me by saying he only needs the file. He doesn't. "You might call Security and escort Lookabaugh out, if he shows up anywhere." He's probably got that covered, too. Well maybe not, since it's Harley. "Don't panic. But if Lookabaugh's there, we can have him arrested. It's a violation of his settlement agreement."

"Yeah," Harley says. "That's kind of what I wanted to know."

"Don't panic." I already said that, and if I say it too much Harley *will* panic. But he already has, judging by the fact that he called me.

I stuff the phone back in my purse, breathe deeply. The skinny girls are still working over their faces. They don't seem to have improved on them much, though.

Back at the table I ignore the merriment, which now

"And then—you could take Sassy's cell phone number," Hilary suggests. "To find out where we've gone when we leave here. We sure can't make this an early night."

"We need to save ourselves so we can dance all night tomorrow night," Laura protests.

"We could *all* go to Vicky's hospital," Kate says brightly.

"No!" Sassy and I say this simultaneously, probably for different reasons.

"Maybe I'll be back," I say. "If not, see you tomorrow."

"Oh, come back, please come back," Kate says. "But in any case, take the limo."

"Twist my arm, will ya? Okay, okay. I'll take the limo. I'll send it back."

"We'll send it back after you. We'll seek you out," Sassy says. "You can run, but you can't hide. We'll find you, wherever you go."

"Whatever you do," Kate says, lifting her glass to me. As I leave, the whole group breaks into the chorus. I can hear them from the street.

wife's $11,000 medical bill, even though she had suffered no ill effects from the surgery.

It's possible this settlement represents some kind of savings—anyway that's the spin I put on it for purposes of my report—because the complaint Lookabaugh filed asked not just for money but, and I quote, "my wife made whole again." Not your typical prayer for relief. I caught some heat, never mind my great track record in preventing off-the-wall settlements. Oh, but that wasn't enough, not for Lookabaugh. No, he has to show up at the hospital, put someone in enough of a panic to call the officer on duty, drag me away from a nice party, and plant his name once again in my boss's mind—right at the end of the fiscal year, when I'm hoping for a raise.

I dig through my purse and realize I don't even have my hospital ID with me. Still, people *do* know me here.

I tell the limo driver not to wait. A blast of cold hospital-scented air hits me as I go through the double doors of Emergency. I don't know why hospital environs are kept so frigid—so the first thing I do is ask one of the Emergency nurses if there's an extra lab jacket around. She eyes my yellow-and-green silk Azzedine Alaia tunic and suggests that I might want to change into scrubs, an idea I dismiss. Wouldn't match my shoes. I reconsider it again when I get to Admin., which is even colder. The hospital could save a big chunk of change by turning the air off in Admin. on the weekends; they could add it to my salary.

Harley, fetchingly attired in a short-sleeved plaid shirt, khaki shorts, black socks, and Birkenstocks, whistles at me. "Wow, Vicky. Makeup and everything! You clean up good."

Harley purses his lip. "We don't know. He may have gone home."

That would be good.

"But we needed your assessment of the situation. As I recall, it wasn't a good situation."

He recalls this because I fell all over myself to write off a fairly large medical bill. The reason I did that was because Lookabaugh scared the shit out of me.

Being a risk manager, I'm not the hardest person to scare. My job, after all, involves assessing potential threats and getting rid of them before they happen and somebody sues the hospital. Not to mention mitigating any damages that have already occurred. The longer I do this, the more peril I see, everywhere.

But it wasn't hard to sense a threat in Peter Lookabaugh. He seemed like at least three different people. The person I saw first was a pleasant country boy with puppy-dog eyes and a kind of aw-shucks shyness, who sounded sincere when he asked things such as, "Could you explain this to me one more time?" Behind this country boy was an evangelist, a silver-tongued angel who claimed the Lord was his copilot and he and the Lord would have to have a little talk about this settlement *thayng* before he could make a decision. Behind the evangelist was a cynical, tough iconoclast, extremely intelligent and well spoken. And mean.

"My assessment? He's a psychopath. He's capable of sustained insanity. He can also act perfectly normal," I say. "And he can be extremely charming and persuasive. So, we've got Security over at L&D? You called the cops?"

sonal hangover preventive. I don't think this second bottle will be enough. I need a jeroboam.

Harley clears his throat. "Well, we don't want him suing us. Again. The other strange thing is that, apparently, first he stopped in Admissions. Or maybe afterward, I'm not sure. Asked for Cindy Hawthorne, didn't say he was looking for a doctor. So the Admissions clerk found a patient named Pamela Hawthorne and gave him her room number, and he wrote it down and thanked her. This was about six-thirty, just before Admissions closed for the night."

"Great." Inwardly I'm groaning. How come Harley didn't say six-thirty when I asked him for a time? "How did we come to find this out?"

"I just found out, right before you walked in. Security went around with his photo, asking if anyone had seen him, and the admissions clerk hadn't left yet and remembered him." And people do remember him. Although not physically intimidating, Lookabaugh throws off something that makes people notice.

"So," I say. "We've got someone from Security at the room of what's her name, Pamela Hawthorne?"

"On the unit," Harley says. "We've got two people from Security over at L&D, in addition to whoever's usually there, and we've got several of them wandering around the hospital looking for the guy. And really, it looks like he left."

"Good work, Harley. And Dr. Hawthorne knows he was around and asking for her? Have you got Security people on her?"

Harley makes a face. "Good idea. I did leave a message at L&D. She's with a patient."

wouldn't be a good idea for Dr. Hawthorne to speak to him."

"Really bad idea," I agree. I don't want to talk to him either. "If he turns up have Security put cuffs on him and call nine-one-one." I sigh. "And call me." So much for deep-sixing the cell phone. This is going to put a damper on my evening, but maybe Lookabaugh won't turn up. Then, with maddening timing, Harley's phone rings.

"Hold off just a second, okay?" Harley hits the button that puts the call on the speakerphone.

"Harley?" says a male voice. "John Abdelbaki, Security. We have here a person claiming to be Barb Lookabaugh, the wife of subject Peter Lookabaugh. She's down here in Emergency. Said she has reason to believe her husband may be in the hospital environs, and reason to believe he may be armed."

that's our code for Labor & Delivery, see, because it's the fourth floor of the Women's Wing—"

I nod and gesture for him to keep going. Faster. I catch myself doing this a lot when I'm on the phone. I don't know if it works even when the person I'm talking to can see me, but John can't and keeps plodding along at the same speed.

"—one over on Medicine, one in the employee parking lot, two on the grounds, one in Emergency and two more who are patrolling, looking out for anyone who's seen this guy."

I can almost see him counting them off on his fingers, and looking uncertain when he's through.

"John, no offense, but our security people aren't really trained for this kind of thing."

"Hell, Vicky, they're armed, at least most of 'em. And it's true that they don't run into situations like this very often, but you gotta face facts, neither do the real cops."

Okay, that tears it. If the person in charge of our security force doesn't think of himself as a real cop—which he's not—then why should I?

"So how about Miz Lookabaugh," John asks. "Should I bring her over to Admin., or where do we want her?"

We want her home, with her husband and children. As long as we're wishing, how about world peace?

Harley and I spend a couple of minutes deciding that Admin.'s probably the best place. At least we're on home turf. I tell John to bring her on up and to make sure his security force is shadowing Dr. Hawthorne. Then I hang up and call the real cops, always a lot of fun. I describe the situation to first one dispatcher (or

sad, and like I said he was kind of sort of depressed already, but not in a bad way, I didn't think, and then he started feeling angry, which he does sometimes, not very often, not that he ever does anything, I mean, he's kind of on a short fuse sometimes and this is one of those times, we've been talking to our priest about it, and I thought we were making progress, and I called him tonight, the priest that is, but still I never thought—"

In order to end a conversation with this woman I sometimes had to be rude. "Barb!" I say. "You said he might be armed, can you tell us about that?"

She responds earnestly. "He's broken things, smashed windows, driven the car into the fence, but he's never hurt anyone. And he's always had this thing about guns, but he's never shot anyone."

"Guns," I say. "Tell me about the guns."

"Well he's not a violent man, not really," she says, no doubt remembering that he threatened Dr. Hawthorne on several occasions and not with financial ruin, although that too was mentioned. "These guns, they're not his, they're more like a collection, in fact they *are* a collection, they were my dad's, they're hanging in a gun rack where they've always been. I mean for years, when I was growing up, but we keep it locked on account of the kids, and anyway it was always locked, even when I was a kid. He, Peter, doesn't hunt or anything. As far as I know, he's never fired a gun, even though he grew up on a ranch, but they weren't into the hunting thing, now I used to be, shot pheasants and things—"

"So he's got a gun with him. What was his thing about guns?"

Barb doesn't gesture or make any unnecessary motions when she talks. She just talks, occasionally nod-

I nod patiently while she keeps going. At least she talks fast. She tells me she called the Weld County police, then went to Peter's desk, where she found a copy of the settlement agreement he had signed. He had ripped it in half.

"But first he, like, scribbled on it," she says. "Almost tore it in half with his pen, like he was revising it, this was a copy and not the original one that he got to keep—"

Like it matters.

"—and so I began to worry, about him, you know, and what he might be thinking, because I have to say, and you know this perfectly well, that upset him, when I had the surgery—"

Don't I ever. "Your little girl," I say. "You said he was talking about your little girl. Which one is that?"

"It's, she's, that's the one we lost, one of the ones we lost, that is, the last one before I, uh, had the surgery. We lost her at twenty weeks but we knew she was a girl, a little girl, and all the rest of them you know are boys, my mom's over there with them now, they're all home. . . ."

The phone rings. As Harley picks it up I realize that, with all of us in here, Harley's office now feels considerably warmer. I try to follow Harley's conversation along with Barb's, but it's hard. She talks even faster and more desperately.

". . . and he's been in such a state, ever since Matt's graduation, because of course this means we're losing one, with no way to make it up, and he got so wound up that I got real afraid he might do something, he sort of focused all his, his feelings, you know, about the

I plunge on, talking almost as fast as Barb Lookabaugh, as if it's contagious. "Mrs. Hawthorne, the patient. She's not Lookabaugh's real target but since our very helpful staff gave out her room number we should move her if she can be moved. If he shows up, it's likely to be over at L&D, and we might have to move people out of there, if their physical condition permits it. When the police come . . ." I pause wondering how many of them will show up and how helpful they'll be, considering that nothing has happened. Harley and John watch me expectantly. Barb babbles.

"You really think we need to move patients?" Harley says. "That's a huge thing—"

"Depends," I say. "You heard her, he might have a gun."

"Only doors unlocked are Emergency," John adds. "And I've got a guy there. This fellow, he can't get in."

"He's already in!"

Harley adds, helpfully, that since he could be anywhere, there's not much point in moving patients from one place to another.

"No, he's looking for Cindy Hawthorne. I think if we don't locate him fairly quickly we should move patients from L&D. And obviously, we should station people at any access point to that floor. There are a lot of them." I'll bet we don't have enough Security people and I can't remember all the ways in. I scrunch up my face to indicate to Harley I'm concentrating. It's hard, what with all the champagne I've had and Barb Lookabaugh nattering along behind me. "The blueprints and all the building and engineering stuff is in my office in big rolls in the corner from when we licensed the new wing. You can use that to make sure we've got all the stairways

shut, having just had a bad thought: What if he's here to grab another baby? Any baby.

"I'm going to L&D *now*," I say. "I don't have my ID. I will be very unhappy, however, if I get onto that floor without anybody asking me for it."

subdued lighting, end tables, magazines, and a box of toys. This area, which was supposed to be user-friendly, is somehow so forbidding that I've never seen anyone on these couches, reading these magazines, or playing with these toys. I think they need to bring in a feng shui consultant. Beyond the waiting area on either side stretch curved halls with even more subdued lighting. Dark and gloomy.

I think the idea was that this desk would be the official nurses' station, but nurses don't take well to being mistaken for receptionists, and also it's a long way from the patients. There's a bell on the desk, and every other time I've come here I've had to ring it. Tonight, the desk is staffed. I gather this is in honor of Lookabaugh. Or maybe in honor of me.

I don't know the nurse, but I can read a name tag as well as the next person, even in subdued light.

"Lydia," I say. "I'm Vicky Lucci, the risk manager. Has anybody talked to you about a situation?"

Lydia snaps her head, tossing long brown bangs out of her face. "Right," she says. "You're the one with no ID. Nice dress."

"Thanks." At least someone alerted her that I'd be coming and wouldn't have an ID. "Anything happening?"

The actual nurses' station is through a hallway behind this desk, and it's still pretty far from the patients. There are a couple of desks with computer terminals and behind them, the whiteboard, which lists all current activity on the unit. I crane my neck but can't see it.

Nurses can be very possessive about their boards. Lydia moves to block my view. "One patient just delivered in 444, which is where Dr.—"

three nights so we're kind of expecting her. Other than that, none that I know of."

"Can we move them?"

Lydia makes a face. It's a lot of work, moving patients. "We're pretty quiet now," she says. "The post deliveries are all stable. I don't think the lady in 446 wants to wait too much longer for her epidural, and the lady in 426 is ready to push."

I shut my eyes and think. Should we remove them? It upsets the patients and it riles the staff. All the rooms here are private, labor-delivery-recovery rooms, or birthing rooms as we often call them. The patients like that and won't get it if they're moved, and that's assuming there's a place to move them to.

But there is. Hospitals have two kinds of beds: actual beds, which are mere pieces of furniture, and staffed beds. Something like 200 beds at Montmorency are unstaffed, hence not counted, but they are pieces of furniture, they are in rooms, and if the staff moves to where the beds are, the beds will be staffed.

The unknown is Peter Lookabaugh. He's tried a lot of different things, some sneaky, some obvious. He's had a couple of hours to get here and either cause some trouble or come to his senses and go home.

"After ten the patients come in through Emergency?"

Lydia nods.

"Let's divert any new patients to General Medicine and move the rest as they're able," I say.

Lydia nods. Once we move some, we have to move them all. She doesn't look happy about it. "I'll pass the word and start getting them ready."

I call Emergency and chat with the head guy down there, developing a plan. Then I call Harley. "Okay.

"Good idea." My heart slows back down to normal. "We're going to get all the patients off this floor for tonight, did Lydia tell you? Just as a precaution. You have anybody that can't be moved?"

Dr. Cynthia Hawthorne shakes her head and looks back over her shoulder.

"Where's the Security guy?" I ask.

She shrugs. "Listen, I just can't talk to Lookabaugh. I'm sorry to wimp out on you like this."

"You don't have to talk to him. Don't worry. You've been through enough."

She sighs.

Lookabaugh filed suit against her, personally, and against the hospital after his wife's surgery, charging medical malpractice. Luckily, he filed *pro se*—probably because he couldn't find an attorney to handle a case with no basis at all. But in addition to filing a huge damage suit, he also began harassing Cynthia, every way he could think of. He told her he planned to return the favor, give *her* a hysterectomy. He told a right-to-life group she was an abortionist and gave them her home address, and they showed up on her sidewalk. He denied doing this. She denied she was an abortionist. Then someone called her office, pretending to be a woman who needed an abortion and asking if she could get one at this office. Dr. Hawthorne's receptionist admitted it was a possibility, at which point the right-to-lifers turned up for another picnic on Cindy's front lawn.

In addition to filing his long, meandering legal briefs with the court, Lookabaugh delivered them to the front seat of Cindy's locked car. Or they appeared in her locker at the hospital.

dicates a certain level of wealth, and these places aren't mortgaged. (Something we check, as a matter of course, whenever Montmorency gets sued.)

Of course the Lookabaughs could be real-estate rich and cash poor. But Barb has also achieved status as a writer of country-and-western songs. For all I know that could pull in more than the tomatoes. Some of her songs have been recorded by big-name stars, and one got so popular it became a crossover hit, and even I heard it. Not only that, I thought it was pretty catchy.

Because I never thought Peter's actions were about the money, I had a bad feeling about settling the case for money, and it wasn't just concern for my budget. On the other hand, I wanted to settle the case. I wanted it to be over.

I guess it's not going to be over until Lookabaugh says it's over.

"Are we really going to have to move the patients?" Cindy asks quietly.

"We've already started." But I've thought about it. What makes the most sense is that Lookabaugh, who knows Dr. Hawthorne delivers babies, will come here if he's after a confrontation. And confrontations seem to be what he's always after.

"There are only eight of them, right?" I ask. "Patients, I mean."

"Yeah," she says tiredly.

"Were you going home?" I ask because Cindy and her partner split calls, alternating days, and they switch at midnight. Which, Cindy says, means often they are both awakened in the night, which wasn't the idea at all.

"I'm the deck doctor tonight, six to six, so no. I don't

"Do you want to wait for the real cops?" She shakes her head and presses the button on the service elevator.

I stand there for a moment wondering if I should go back and meet the cops in Admin. I decide to stay put and help move the patients, if they need me. I stroll down the hall, looking into the rooms. Unlike the reception area, they do look kind of homey. They don't have carpeting but they have wood floors, rag rugs, rocking chairs, VCRs, and Jacuzzis. Apparently, Jacuzzis help—a lot. The high-tech equipment is disguised in cabinets or, in the case of the delivery beds, camouflaged with patchwork quilts. Patients who need intervention are quickly wheeled down to the operating rooms, right behind the main elevators.

This building is almost oval, bisected in the center by a hallway with elevators on one side, two operating rooms on the other. The service elevator in the nursing station opens on both sides—on one side into this area, on the other, into the hall. I walk through the elevator when it opens—a shortcut—then stroll along the oval—known informally, and inevitably, as the Ovary.

I don't see any signs of evacuation, but I do pass a pregnant woman, supported by a man and a woman—her husband and her midwife, I assume. She takes two steps, stops, rubs her back, takes two more steps. "This hall is *boring*," she whines as I pass. "Who the fuck designed such a goddamned *boring* building?"

I'd like to point out that it could be worse; the halls could be straight. Over in General Medicine the halls *are* straight. And at least we have art, in the form of Barbara Froula prints of Denver scenes.

"Labor is boring. I want an ice cream cone. Could

I glance through the window, then do a double take. Swallow hard. Try to keep myself from my instinctive reaction, which is to flee.

How did everybody miss this? Lookabaugh is in the nursery! Pointing something long that looks like a gun at the baby nurse!

He's seen me, too. Holding the gun in position with one hand, he raises the other and waves, then motions me inside.

I wonder desperately whether joining them is something I should do. I don't seem to have much choice. At least whatever's going to happen will happen fast—because the cops are on the way.

"Miss Vicky." Lookabaugh always called me that. It drove me nuts. "It's been a long time."

"Not long enough," I say.

In my peripheral vision I see the nurse express something—terror, outrage, who knows. Like she thinks he's going to shoot her for my snide comment about it being not long enough. I was a little surprised to hear it myself. Maybe subconsciously I thought it would be bad to show fear.

Somewhere in my attorney-work-product privileged notes, I have written that Peter Lookabaugh is smarter than he looks. Not that he looks dumb. No—he looks cute, sometimes even puppy-dog cute. He looks like a high-school student, even though he's got to be close to forty. This illusion is furthered tonight by his letter jacket.

I don't know what he could possibly have lettered in, since he's slight. Maybe manipulation and intimidation. He's obviously lost a lot of weight and maybe shrunk, since earning this jacket. Or maybe he stole it.

"How long have you been here?" I ask, studying him to see which persona I'm dealing with right now. He looks back, seeming both amused and perplexed. The corners of his mouth turn up even when he's not smiling. His eyebrows are heavy, dark, and curve around his eyes like they're sliding off his face, making him look naive rather than crafty. But when he raises them, as he does when I come into the room, he looks almost satanic.

He replies without answering my question.

"You got a good gal here," he says, grinning. "I came in and offered to let her go if I could shoot one of the babies. She said no."

He nods.

"You weren't ever supposed to come here again. Do you remember that?" He nods.

"As a patient," he says craftily. "I agreed not to voluntarily seek treatment here. I'm not seeking treatment."

"No? Then why are you here? Treatment is what we do."

"Butchery, is what you do."

"Peter." I stop. I was going to go into a rhapsody about how babies were born here, but he knows that; that's why he's here.

"But I guess we can talk," he says. "While we wait for the butcher to show up. You know traditionally doctors were lower than butchers. They were barbers, which is from the same root as 'barbarous,' and it's easy to see why. At one time real doctors looked down upon doctors who cut. Actually they didn't cut—they sawed, they chopped. In fact they still do, don't they? You bet they do."

"Your wife was hemorrhaging. The doctor saved her life."

He ignores me. "Anyway, the ones who practiced medicine, the *healers*, they considered themselves a whole other class from the barbers and butchers. As well they should."

I wonder if he knows that here at Montmorency Medical Center, the medical chief of staff outranks the chief of surgery. Well, he won't hear it from me.

"I can't talk to someone who's holding a gun on somebody anyway," I say.

"Not a problem," he says. "I think I'm about all talked out."

comes in . . . well goddamnit she knows better than that . . . yeah, right, sorry . . . no, it was a slip, I don't talk that way around the kids. . . ."

Is this the same guy who threatened to shoot a newborn baby? Deferring to his mother—no, I guess that would be Barb's mother—on the subject of cussing around his kids? Is he softening? Could I do something here? Too late. He hangs up.

"Okay," he says to me. "I guess she could be here. She's not home. Now I need to find that doctor!"

"She knows that," I say. "She left the hospital as soon as she heard you were here." I try to convince myself that I am a good liar, and actually, I'm not bad. Better on the phone, but you can't have everything.

"I get the feeling you're not being truthful with me," he says, nudging me with the end of the gun. "I get the very strong sense that she *is* here, on this very floor. Close."

I can barely breathe but I squeeze out a few words. "She was alerted that you were here."

"I thought it seemed mighty quiet up here. Not like when I was here before. But I'm the kind of person needs to be convinced. So let's take a walk."

Without moving the gun away from me he motions at the door. I feel a thrill of relief and realize I'm sweating like a horse. This will get him out of here, outside, where the cops can get him. Maybe. Have the patients been cleared off the floor? I've lost awareness of everything but this room.

I start for the door. "Just a minute," he says. "We're all going. You and me and this lady"—he waves the gun toward the scared nurse—"and the babies."

a clue. He's going to do the opposite of what I want him to do. So I wheel the isolette around and catch just a glimpse of the nurse. Brief eye contact, during which I try to signal her to break away if she can. Too bad we don't both know sign language.

I push the isolette along, going slowly, listening to the wheels squeak and feeling the gun between my shoulder blades. Whirling through my head are several concerns, like: what if the mother of one of these babies comes to the nursery to get him? What if a mother who has her baby in her room brings the baby back to the nursery? Where is the woman who was walking the halls? How am I going to get out of this? *Where are the cops!?*

We stroll about halfway around the oval, almost to the elevators, when the quiet hum of the air conditioners goes off, a sound I wasn't even aware of until it stopped. Does this mean something? And if so, what? Probably it means nothing. Probably these things are on some kind of timer.

"Turn here," Lookabaugh says. We make a right at the elevators, crossing to the other side as if we're making a gigantic figure eight. I pass the elevators and veer left, expecting Lookabaugh to turn me back the other way, as he did before. He doesn't.

Plodding through the halls in my four-inch heels could get tedious pretty quickly. It's already tedious, in fact. *Where are the cops?* Did they get lost, or are they somewhere formulating a plan? I grab onto that. They're here, and turning off the air conditioning was part of their plan, although I can't think how it would help.

We pass the deserted reception area. Lookabaugh, who hasn't said anything this whole quarter-lap, stops

tirely convinced some people *can't* read your mind. Like the woman who's suing us, saying she lost her psychic powers after having a CT scan following an auto accident. She's got a tough case, because first she will have to prove she actually *had* psychic powers—

"Dr. Hawthorne," shrieks the intercom right above my head, "report to Room 4426. Dr. Cynthia Hawthorne, Room 4426, please." The message perplexes me.

It's a female voice or I would have suspected Lookabaugh. But he's looking fixedly at me. If he's reading either my mind or my body language, he knows I'm completely confused. Is this a trap to get him to that room? I hope so, but I don't know.

At any rate I am one hundred percent certain that Dr. Hawthorne, hearing this, will *not* go there. I've no sooner thought this than Lookabaugh says, "So, let's go to that room, right? What was it, 4426? Lead the way."

"If we had the security cameras hooked up," Harley said, "Then we'd know exactly where they are." He looked around the Admin. reception area, which was filling up with various people, all cops, in uniform and otherwise. "Or if they'd only stay in one place for a while. Long enough for us to get the patients out. What did they say?"

The cop wearing headphones shook his head and squinted his eyes before answering. "They came out of the nursery. Two women pushing those bassinet things and one guy, armed. Our guys ducked out of the way just in time."

"Why can't they—you—do something?" Harley

The cop signaled for silence and listened intently, shaking his head almost imperceptibly. "This isn't helping much," he said after a minute. "It was a good idea to hook into the intercom but we need something a little more sensitive."

Harley swallowed. "I've got a phone technician on the way. As soon as he can get here—it being Friday night, and all—"

"Yeah, we've got a tech on the way ourselves," the cop said. "All's I'm picking up is things like, 'the other way,' and 'stop.' Sounds like he wants to stay in one place for a minute himself. Gimme that floor plan." As Harley reached for the drawing over the receptionist's desk, the cop changed his mind. "Naw, leave it there, I'll come over."

"The mother is hysterical," Taffy reported calmly. "Dr. Hawthorne is with her but she's maybe getting violent."

"Great," Harley said. "Maybe Dr. Hawthorne would have preferred to take her chances with Lookabaugh, instead of calming down the mother of a kidnapped brand-new baby. I sure would."

"There's four patients and three nurses left on the unit," Taffy said. "They had to take the last patient down the stairs, because the guy, Lookabaugh, went into the nurses' lounge, where the service elevator is."

Two of the cops spread out the floor plan and zeroed in on the lounge. "Elevator here," one of them said.

"It's big," Taffy said helpfully. "And the great thing? It doesn't ding when it stops."

"That might be handy," the cop mused. He picked up a small phone and spoke into it, conveying that in-

6

"Room 4426," Peter says again. "Is that on this floor?"

It sounds like it's on the 44th floor, or would to anyone unfamiliar with the hospital's numbering system. No two rooms in the Montmorency complex have the same numbers, for safety reasons. To those of us in the know, 4426 means room 426 in building number four. This building. This floor.

It's possible I could herd him out of here and somewhere else, if I knew of a place that would be better. Since I don't, I see no particular benefit and a certain amount of danger in leading Peter around the hospital. Particularly if the police set the page up in order to lure him to that room.

"Follow me," I say.

"No," he says.

"Okay. Go straight out and turn left." *Go directly to hell. Do not pass Go. . . .* And the babies and I, and their nurse, can stay right here. Take the elevator down as soon as he leaves.

Peter realizes this as soon as I do. "You go ahead," he says, almost grudgingly. "Like before."

Like before, he plants the gun's muzzle, or whatever

bed; a tall young man with sandy hair and a scraggly red beard; a dark-skinned nurse, who starts forward, then sees Lookabaugh's gun, and stops with her mouth open.

"God damn," I whisper.

"The doctor's not here," Lookabaugh accuses.

"He's not the doctor," the patient says.

"You people should not be here," the nurse says. She moves between us and the patient, who's propped in the bed with her knees up and her husband (I assume) at her shoulder.

"Who the hell are they?" the husband asks. "Where's the doctor?"

I wonder if introductions are in order. I step back. I hear Lookabaugh breathing behind me. Behind him, the door eases shut. And latches.

"What the hell?" He backtracks to the door, pushes against it, then cranks the handle. I give a mental thumbs up to the neonatal nurse. "Shit, what is this?"

He rattles the knob, then pulls the door. It opens about an inch, just enough to reveal one of the iso-lettes—empty—sort of hanging on the outside door latch. Peter yanks on the door again, there's a clatter, and the door opens a little farther. He sticks the gun out, fires twice, then slams the door shut and turns to me.

I am breathless and deaf. "Peter," I say, trying to remain on my feet. Did he hit anyone? Did he even aim? "Don't shoot, shooting's not—" I stop, because he already shot. And also because, even though I heard my voice echo in my ears, I'm not sure I spoke loudly enough for Peter to hear me.

"That'll catch someone's attention," I mutter.

"We shouldn't be here," I say to Peter, the understatement of the century. His face is glistening with sweat. "You shouldn't be here. Why are you doing this? What do you want? You can see for yourself, the doctor isn't here."

"Yeah," he says in a faraway voice, and starts roaming the room—which is small—opening cabinet doors as if he expects Dr. Hawthorne to be hiding behind one of them.

Arden, the nurse, moves over, checks the IV pole that's still standing, and shakes her head. I reconstruct what just happened: The first pole, falling, disconnected the second one. The first one was probably delivering fluids, or possibly antibiotics or a labor-inducing drug like Pitocin. The second one, sturdier, was providing epidural painkillers to the patient.

"Breathe, girl," Arden tells her patient. "Keep breathing. Take a big breath here." She turns to me and confirms what I've guessed. "Looks like we've lost the epidural catheter. Now we had it down at a pretty low level anyway, so she could work with the contractions."

Peter slams cabinet doors shut. I can't think of any way for us all to escape while he's distracted, because he's not *that* distracted.

"I paged the doctor," Arden says in a low voice. "This is Deanna's birthday and she thought it would be neat if her baby was born today, so we were going for an episiotomy. But I guess we aren't going to make it. She's probably got another hour or so of pushing."

I am not an overly emotional person but it's all I can do not to burst into tears. Is this a sane person speaking? A wild man just came in, fired a gun twice out the hall and twice in the room, and Arden stands here,

The husband gets paler and Deanna lets his arm go.

"What's your name?" Peter demands.

"Uh . . . Alexi."

"Okay, uh-Alexi, get on with it. It's a black case. An attaché, you know what that is? Like a suitcase, only smaller. With a handle on it. By the nurses' station. Sitting on the floor. I do appreciate your doing this." Alexi backs around the corner to the door, with one last anguished look at his wife. The isolettes in the hall clatter as Alexi pushes them out of the way.

"Now then," Peter says to me, in a very calm and rational voice. "You need to call your people and tell them I've got enough dynamite to blow this building and everyone in it to kingdom come, and I'll do it if that doctor doesn't get her ass up here."

"How'm I supposed to do that? You shot the phone."

He looks blank for a moment. I remind myself that's just the thing with his eyebrows. "Open the window," he says. "Yell it out the window."

"These windows don't open."

"Bullshit. Pull the curtain."

Arden moves toward the cord that controls the curtain.

"Not her. You, Miss Vicky."

I step over and pull the curtain. "See? No way to open it." I've barely gotten the words out when he takes the larger gun, aims it at the window, and fires.

This time, Deanna does scream. The nurse grimaces, and I fall back against the wall. My ears clench shut with the noise. The only reason I know I'm not deaf is I can still hear the thumping of my heart. Lookabaugh

7

He couldn't find the goddamned suitcase anyplace. When he heard the shots he turned and ran as fast as he could back to the one place, the only place they could have come from. He'd kill the motherfucker! He'd fucking kill him! He'd tackle him, pound his head against the floor, it didn't matter the son-of-a-bitch had two guns, he'd kill him with his bare hands—

Hands came out of nowhere and grabbed him, stopped him in midstride. Now what the fuck? He lashed out with an elbow, aimed a kick. "Nooooo!" he howled. Someone grabbed him in a headlock and clamped a gloved hand over his mouth.

Harley heard the shots through the headphones, which he had picked up when the big cop got another, smaller set. "My God!" he yelled. "He's killed them!"

Nobody paid the slightest attention. Nobody had said a word to him since the big cop had introduced the hostage negotiators. After that Harley watched the entire scene slip out of his control. Not that it had ever been under his control, but he'd felt in charge up to that point. For instance, when he'd explained how he knew the page for the doctor had been initiated by an insider,

now!" she ordered in a strident voice that cut through the room like a dentist's drill. Even from four feet away Harley could hear the crackly reply.

"He won't come. Says they'll kill his wife if he's not back in five minutes and he's supposed to bring something . . ."

"We need to talk to him."

"He's not the shooter. He's—his wife's the patient. Who's in labor."

Harley felt his guts twist and his shoulders trying to sag, and resisted. A weirdo on the premises, newborn babies taken hostage, shots fired, now a woman in labor being threatened. What next?

"You know the policy," Chopak said into her handset. "Once someone exits from a hostage situation they don't go back. That makes it look like we're doing an exchange."

This time Harley couldn't hear the reply.

Taffy tapped him on the shoulder. "Good news," she said. "The neonatal nurse got the two babies away, and they've been reunited with their mothers." Taffy seemed to be enjoying this episode. But maybe she was just happy that the newborns were safe.

Harley opened his mouth, then nodded at Taffy. "How'd she get them away?"

"Just grabbed them and ran, sounds like."

Turlow turned to her. "I want to talk to that nurse," he said. "Real quick."

Taffy, still holding the phone, spoke into it again.

"We'll send someone over for her," Turlow said. Taffy nodded.

Harley straightened his shoulders and leaned back in his chair, waiting for someone to ask him where General

hospital right now, I say, let him go back. Cover him, or whatever, but if he loses his wife and baby because he didn't go back, because you wouldn't let him go back, there's gonna be hell to pay, and you are going to pay it!"

"I don't have time for this," Chopak said. She turned to her husband. "Explain it to him."

"Just a second, Sue," her husband said. "This is a different kind of situation, and the gunman hasn't actually harmed anyone yet. And the squad wants to let him go back, right?"

"We don't know what's going on in that room right now," she said. "That's the point. If we let the guy go back in, we lose leverage with the suspect, before we've even made contact."

Swartz looked at his watch. "How long have we got?"

"About a minute and a half!" Chopak said.

"Show of good faith on our part," Swartz said, negotiating, as far as Harley could see, with his own wife. "Plus, the gunman doesn't know we have people on the scene."

"He will if this guy goes back in. What about the suitcase?"

Swartz shook his head. "The suspect knows there was no suitcase. It was a test. A setup. The hostage has to go back to his wife. It's what anybody would do. And it won't hurt if the suspect knows we're on the scene. It's probably what he wants."

Harley began to see why they worked in teams.

"It could be just an excuse to shoot," Chopak said. But she spoke into her handheld again. "Okay. Our take

"No big deal having babies," Lookabaugh says. "My wife and I've had eight of them. Should have been more."

Deanna gulps, swallows, and sobs.

Arden chooses to pretend Lookabaugh isn't in the room. "Can you feel those contractions?" she asks. "You'll feel one in a minute." Then she turns to me. "These epidurals, you get a whole different birth experience. Used to be women were crying to push, and they *pushed*."

"It's a natural process," Lookabaugh says. "It happens when it happens."

Thank *you*, Mr. Expert.

Deanna tangles her hands in the sheet then buries her face in it.

Arden speaks to her patient but motions to me. "We're on track for a perfect delivery here. Everything's going well. Let's just get you up a bit, into a better pushing position."

Taking my cue, I move around to the other side of the bed, to lift Deanna into a more upright position. I haven't done actual nursing in years and I was never an obstetrical nurse, although I did a rotation in OB while in training. I still remember how to position a patient.

"It'll help if you put your knees up and grab onto these handholds," Arden tells Deanna gently. "Now, I'll tell you when to start pushing. You feeling the contractions still?"

Deanna shuts her eyes tightly, squeezing tears out, and moves her mouth a few times before actual words emerge. "A little. I can feel a little."

"Feel like you need to push?"

Arden switches on the light over the bed, a three-way bulb. It bathes the room in thin yellow light. "Eleven-forty."

"So I could still . . ." Deanna trails off. "Has it been five minutes?"

"Not yet," Arden says. "Don't watch the clock. Get ready, here's another one. Cleansing breath!"

Arden and I both know Deanna wasn't talking about the timing of the contraction. I have to admire the way she handled it.

I should have offered some encouragement to Deanna. My obstetrical rotation comes back to me, particularly the bit in orientation where the head nurse told us, a bunch of women who have never been pregnant (nonparas), how hard labor could be. "We tell the mothers this," she said. "That going through labor is like somebody telling you to move an enormous weight, a piano for instance, from your living room, down three steps to the sidewalk, out to the street, and then pick it up and put it in a truck. All by yourself. We can't help them, but we can stand on the sidelines and offer encouragement. That's what we tell them, and that's why we're telling you. That's how hard it can seem to them. Impossible." We nodded, not really comprehending. "But then we also tell them not to worry, because at the last stage, putting the piano up on the truck, they'll develop the strength of a superhero and they'll be able to do it. But you, on the sidelines, it won't look all that hard to you. It is. Believe it. Give them all the encouragement you can."

Naturally after this buildup the first delivery I attended looked very easy indeed. Three pushes and *whoosh*, a multipara who didn't need any encourage-

8

"We got zip on this guy, right?" Turlow said to the uniformed woman.

"Just traffic," the woman said, responding to Turlow but speaking to the hostage negotiators. "Following too close, 1992, failure to yield, 1994, got points, paid fine. He's a solid citizen."

Harley frowned. By now he knew the weedy-looking woman in uniform—M. J. Robbins—was part of the backup negotiation team, sort of a trainee, dedicated to running down information that the negotiators needed and learning the ropes. And keeping people like Harley out of the negotiators' way, which Robbins did by explaining a great many things he'd never considered about hostage negotiators. They worked with the SWAT team but were not part of it. He knew they considered all hostages as goners but hoped to win them back, either one at a time or all at once, and that unless something new developed they would try to talk the suspect out, rather than letting the SWAT team stage a commando action.

Harley favored a commando action himself, only if it was successful, of course, but nobody'd asked him. Still,

against the bullhorn idea. Ask them to go with some-thing a little more subtle.

They had taken all sorts of measures he wouldn't have expected. Sent a team out to Lookabaugh's house, for instance, with a search warrant. What good was that? The guy was *here*.

"Hey," Harley said, remembering something from Barb Lookabaugh's stream-of-consciousness babbling. "His wife said he'd pulled out the settlement agreement and had it sitting on his desk, all marked up. Um, scrib-bled on and then ripped up, she said."

"Okay, good," Chopak said. "Anything else? Like what might have prompted this incident?"

"The oldest son graduated from high school," Har-ley said. "He's been depressed. The father, that is, not the son. Under the black dog, she called it."

"That's a new one," Chopak said. "Did he say what he wanted?"

"Over and over," Harley replied. "He wants the doc-tor. And he wants his wife made whole again."

"You talked to him?"

"That's what he's always said he wanted."

She frowned.

"And what *we* want," Harley added, "is this guy out of our hospital and out of our hair, forever. Whatever it takes."

Under cover of the noise of the television, Deanna whispers, "Isn't this baby safer inside me?"

"Not now," Arden whispers back. "It's time for her."

I remember it was a little girl the Lookabaughs lost and suggest, "Call it *him*."

maybe it was a shopping bag from Kmart. But that's not the point. The point is, you didn't get it."

Sounds to me like there was no bag, which is good news in a way, and bad news in another way. I knew Peter was crazy, but this sounds like he's totally lost touch with reality. I start to move around the curtain— to do what, I'm not sure. Alexi is still in the doorway. In the dim lighting of the room, his face glows white. Well, he wouldn't be the first father to faint in the delivery room.

"Shut the door," Lookabaugh orders. Alexi pushes it shut behind him, then rushes past me to his wife. Lookabaugh keeps the gun aimed at the door.

"Hey, just a minute. If you all go back there, I'll start to get scared that you're conspiring against me."

I muffle a nervous snort. *Scared?* Right, we're a big threat here.

"Besides," Lookabaugh says, "I get to feeling lonely."

We've all been pretending the curtain separates us from Lookabaugh, and therefore, what happens on his side has no bearing on what transpires on this side. Or at least, I have been.

"I'll come out," I say, shattering the nonexistent sound barrier. I turn to Deanna. "That way, Alexi will be able to see *him* being born." A subtle reminder that we've just changed the sex of their child.

I miss the no doubt tender husband-wife reunion but hear Arden's continuing instruction to push *now*.

"If the nurse needs me," I say, unable to think of any reason she would, "then I guess Alexi will come back out, so you'll know we aren't conspiring—"

"Shut up!" Lookabaugh doesn't move. In the flicker-

"Doesn't sound too good either way," Harley said.

"Well, no." Robbins flashed him that smile again. "On the other hand, if they have a plan to take hostages, then part of that plan includes communication with people who can give them what they want, so they want to initiate contact. The ones who just end up accidentally with hostages, they might panic. We don't want panic."

Harley nodded as if he understood.

"Takes patience in either case. You can't rush things."

Harley sat back in his chair. "So how long could this take?"

"The longer the better," Robbins said. "For the safety of the hostages, that is. Count on three to six hours at a minimum."

"So it could be *morning*," he groaned. Robbins nodded.

Once inside the bathroom, I wonder why I didn't think of this earlier. Between all the champagne, the water, and the hastily gulped coffee, it's a wonder I haven't wet my pants. But getting out of Peter Lookabaugh's gaze is downright refreshing. I shut the door. He doesn't stop me. I turn on the light. Does he know these doors don't lock from the inside? Probably. I wish they did.

I remove a plastic insert, used to collect and measure the patient's urine. I suppose I once knew why we do this but I've forgotten. At any rate I conscientiously preserve Deanna's output (several cc's) by placing the container under the sink. Then I sit—and quite aside from the relief to my bladder, I've been on my feet for hours. I gaze longingly at the Jacuzzi. Wouldn't that feel nice,

Taliaferro, whose last name looked like it could fly but who pronounced it "Tolliver"—much clunkier. Or a college friend who married a guy called "Dottery," and I didn't realize until I got the wedding announcement it was spelled "Daugherty."

A couple of meetings after correcting my name, Peter took the first draft of his settlement agreement— stamped DRAFT and with redlined corrections—and signed it with a flourish. I wasn't going to complain. Signed is signed, after all. I immediately noted, while bearing it triumphantly to the copy machine, that he had not signed his own name. Took me another forty-five minutes to realize that "Walt A. Yenrotta" was attorney-at-law, backwards.

After that, things seriously deteriorated.

Well—If I sit here and remember every time Peter Lookabaugh pissed me off I'll lose my temper and go out and throw something at him. I put all my pent-up anger into flushing the toilet. Since it's a push-button flush, this means I punch it very hard. Not terribly satisfying. It doesn't cry or anything. Then I get ready to open the door, to face a man who might conceivably blow me into small pieces when I come out.

Maybe he'll let me have a last cigarette.

fourth floor of the women's wing routed to the four phones on the four desks in the reception area. Harley waited for Turlow to ask him where the wiring for those phones was, but Turlow didn't. Neither did the young guy. He just said, "Check," and went off with his tool belt clanking.

Harley glanced at his watch. Getting on toward midnight, and until recently that would have meant that some other hospital official would take over the pager. Not anymore. Vicky had convinced Harley that midnight was a bad time for a switchover. She'd pointed out that in the case of an all-night situation, this would mean two vice presidents getting interrupted and losing sleep instead of just one.

And damn the luck, it had to be him. He had a dozen fine and eager vice presidents, and he'd drawn the rotation for this weekend. A lot of COOs wouldn't even *be* in the rotation. In fact, he recalled switching with Vicky. Was it Vicky he'd switched with, or somebody else? Hell, it didn't matter—he was here. And so was Vicky. And he guessed he could feel guilty about calling her, but how was he to know she'd come charging down here? All he'd wanted was to find Lookabaugh's file.

Just as well, though, because he bet that almost any of those junior veeps would have called him anyway, knowing he liked to be the one in charge.

The phones on the four desks started ringing, one after another. Turlow put one of them on speakerphone. "Check," he said into it. "They're all ringing."

"Just a minute here," Harley said. "Hospital calls come in on these phones." He was ignoring the fact that during normal weekend operations no one was in these

I step across the floor as softly as my clunky shoes will let me. If Lookabaugh did go to sleep, that would be good.

A loud "Aargh!" comes from behind the curtain. Well, shit! Here I am, tiptoeing across the floor so Peter Lookabaugh can nod off and we can all get out of this, and then Deanna lets out this howl. Apparently her epidural has worn off enough to enable her to feel the contractions. Selfish bitch.

Whoa! I'm getting as nutty as Lookabaugh.

Anyway, he's not asleep. He sits there, piggishly, in the only chair on this side of the curtain, and I really, really want to sit down. Lie down. Go off to dreamland myself. What with all the partying, the drinking, and the late-night gab fests, wink for wink he's probably ahead of me even if he has been up for three days.

I consider sinking down to the floor, the only place left to sit. No, by god, I'll stay on my feet all night before I'll do that—sit at his feet like a dog. He seems like the kind of guy who would like that.

Deanna lets out another yelp, and Arden tells her she's doing great as Alexi counts out the seconds. Which seem to be going by awfully slowly. Probably even more so for Deanna.

I lean against the wall, wondering what on earth got into Lookabaugh—why this month and not last? Why tonight, not last week? I pull out of my memory everything I can remember about the situation. He and Barb were high school sweethearts, married young, had kids. . . . My mind drifts into a different direction. What's wrong with me? Here's this madman, who's been married twenty years, nice and stable, and I can't keep anything going more than four months. Yeesh.

a little nuts babysitting my brother's kids for the weekend, and there are only four of them, and it's only for the weekend. My mother had four of us, too, and she's only a little deranged. Somewhat.

Even assuming Barb is also somewhat deranged by being around all those children, or even some of them, I would think if she got a clue her husband was gung ho nutso, she would pack her bags and hit the road, Jack. Or at least stop procreating so that, at some later point, she *could* get away from him.

But that's what she *did*—stopped having children. Aha. The brilliant Lucci brain finally takes hold and digs in. Wife stops having children, husband goes bonkers.

I go back to what I know about them, once again, and conclude that this problem first came up a few months after Barb lost her baby. Which was, most likely, Barb's due date. Approximately a year ago. That makes sense. So the current crisis might very well be in response to what would have been the baby's first birthday. Maybe Barb got depressed? And her loyal and protective husband took decisive action?

No, Vicky, *no*. Back to the drawing board. Do not, repeat, *do not* blame the wife for the fact that the husband is sitting here with two guns and—is he snoring? If so I could probably get to the guns. . . . no. The noise I heard came from Deanna and was more on the order of moan mingled with gasping cough.

I have to straighten out my thinking. A loyal and protective husband would not arrive at a hospital with guns and terror. He is wacko. It isn't Barb's fault.

A little more of Barb's song trickles into my brain. It was one of those crossover hits, basically country but it

Like they hadn't even listened to him. "Those aren't *our* helicopters," Harley said to Robbins, because she was the closest. And because she seemed to have been designated the person to hold his hand, so to speak.

Robbins shrugged. "They aren't ours either. Trust me."

"The media," Harley said.

"Probably." They listened a moment and the sound of rotors receded. "Or some other hospital around here. Or maybe it is ours. Believe me, the guys love to trot out that helicopter. But they didn't tell us, and we're not in communication."

Harley twitched his shoulders to relieve tension. "Just what do you people do, anyway? I mean, how are you making this situation better?"

Robbins didn't exactly frown, but her general expression was kind of downturned and sour. "For one thing it's contained. He won't be taking any more hostages."

"Yeah, okay. That's one thing."

"For another thing, we can try to establish contact here. Let the suspect know there are resources."

"Let him know he has us by the short hairs, in other words."

Robbins flashed Harley a sly kind of look, almost amused. She held the earphones up to one ear, listening as she talked to Harley. "We can let him think that."

He wondered what she was listening to. Somebody telling her the helicopter was, in fact, sent to assist the SWAT team, maybe. "Seriously, if he wanted to talk, believe me, we've talked. Vicky has talked to him many times and had even gotten him to sign a settlement.

wants, or even cares about. It becomes like a game you're playing with each other, to get to this point. Ah, it's hard to explain. It's like at a certain point, you start cooperating with each other. Like haggling. When you get to that point, things almost always work out."

"Hmmm," Harley said. Skeptical.

"All right, when I know this better I'll be better at explaining it. You say, okay, what do you want? And the suspect will say, maybe, that he wants a helicopter so he can fly to Cuba. Now this is ridiculous, because I don't think a helicopter can even make it that far."

"Certainly not from Denver," Harley said.

"Yeah. If we were in Florida. . . . No, but he says that, and you say, 'Well, I can't promise you a helicopter, but let me talk to my boss.' "

"Like the used car salesman who has to talk to his manager."

"Exactly," Robbins said. "Or even the new car salesman. And so you know what happens next."

"A slight delay." Harley nodded.

"Right. And then you come back. 'Well, we can't do a helicopter, what about a car?' And so on. You get a certain rhythm going. Understanding that none of this means anything about what's *really* going on. Now Swartz is really good at getting at the subtext of things. He can sense things. But what it comes down to, what most of these people want is attention. They're jammed up. You can't really solve their problems, and even if you could, they've just made them a hell of a lot worse. So you look to other things. Like what kind of car they'll get, instead of a helicopter."

"Money?" Harley asked. Thinking of his budget. Or rather, Vicky's budget.

you signed an agreement saying you wouldn't do that any more, and you wouldn't come here any more, and now here you are. I mean, why are you here?"

There's a long silence from Peter, during which time I hear Arden talking about transition breathing and Deanna, obviously muffling her moans.

"I mean, what on earth could you possibly hope to accomplish, coming here like this? What's the story?"

At last he answers. "The story."

"Yeah. What—how can I phrase this? What's your problem here?" Meanwhile I'm thinking *transition* breathing? I thought that was different from push breathing. I guess I thought she was closer to delivery and, boy, I hope she's not having problems. A breech, or the cord wrapped around the neck, or any of the other things that could necessitate a C-section.

Peter's voice comes out of the darkness with force. "My problem is that, whenever I get something good going, somebody comes along and fucks it up." A long silence, from everybody, hangs shimmering in the air to punctuate his words.

"Well . . ."

"I lost my ranch, that I grew up on," he says. "Lost my parents. Lost my fucking inheritance, man. Now I'm losing my family."

"You're not." I'm so tired that my thoughts are spinning around on three levels that seem equally valid. On one level I want to say, "So play a country-and-western song backwards, Peter." On another I think I could almost relate to the loss issues because couldn't we all. And on the third level Barb must have been lying about his not knowing much about guns. Every ranch kid I

"You didn't need to know," Chopak snapped.

"That's how we know what's going on," Robbins explained. "Only, really, we don't. See, the SWAT tech just stuck it in the guy's pocket before they let him go back in the room. He doesn't know it's there."

"He *probably* doesn't know it's there," Chopak corrected.

"So we're recording these people without their consent," Harley said.

"We're listening, not recording," Robbins said. "Problem with this kind of mike is, if you know you're wearing it, you can accommodate, but he doesn't know it. It's in his pocket, there's scratchy sounds, and basically all we're getting is his wife screaming, which is kind of hard to listen to, but we have to."

"Not the worst thing we could be hearing," Chopak pointed out.

Harley leaned forward. "She's screaming? What's he doing to her?"

"She's having a baby," Robbins said. "We haven't heard anything from the suspect at all."

"You think he's still there?"

"Oh yeah. If he left the room, believe me, we'd have heard about that. And not on the remote mike."

"We need to make contact," Chopak said. "But, as you can see, we're monitoring the situation. And this does not seem like a good time."

Harley sat back, barely mollified. The night was ticking away. Crime-scene tape surrounded parts of his hospital. The helicopter flying around probably belonged to one of the TV stations and probably contained cameras—but, luckily, it was still the middle of the night, so

Barb Lookabaugh bounded through the door. "I needed to find a phone," she said. "You know, I had to call my mother, she's looking after the kids, she'd want to know what was happening, and she said we're on the news, and then I had to go down to the car for something, and couldn't remember where I was parked, and then I thought maybe if I went over to where Peter was, only I didn't exactly know where that was, but I asked one of the cops, because they're everywhere, and he told me to get lost, which I pretty much already was. But I really think if I could just talk to him, he's not a bad person at heart, and—"

Chopak, Swartz, and Robbins formed a circle around her, all talking at once. "Your husband's really in some trouble. . . ." "Has he ever had any psychological problems?" "What kind of weapons did he bring?" "Any alcohol or substance abuse?" Barb stopped talking and looked like she was going to start crying again. Harley took the opportunity to pick up the headphone that Robbins had dropped. It seemed like somebody should be monitoring the situation. It didn't take long to see why she'd dropped it. All he heard was a world-class scream.

"I can't do this!" Deanna yells. "It's too hard, it's too much!"

"Breathe!" Arden orders. "Atta girl . . . big cleansing breath . . . now push . . . here it comes . . . a couple more pushes like this and you'll have . . . him . . ."

I wonder if Lookabaugh noticed how she hesitated before saying "him." It seemed obvious to me, but then, I know Deanna's expecting a girl.

Lookabaugh seems oblivious, staring at the ceiling

your epidural for the worst of it, lady, that's all I can say. All you have to do now is push that baby out." He aims the gun in the vicinity of Alexi's head. "So do it!" He punctuates each word by stabbing with the gun. "You! Have! That! Baby! Now!"

think? What kind of woman would stay with somebody who did something like this? Huh? You are one sick piece of shit, and if she didn't know it before she'll know it now—won't she."

Harley was the only one listening through the headphones to hear Lookabaugh's threat, and at that moment he wished it was being recorded as well as transmitted. If anybody ever needed evidence to lock this guy up forever, here it was. "Hey," he yelled at the negotiators, who were still talking to Barb Lookabaugh. He suspected they had some fancy term for it, like debriefing. "Something's happening." What a mess. Something happening, and he was the only one picking it up. "Someone should hear this!"

Robbins came over and grabbed the headphones. "The SWAT commander's listening too," she said. "Hold on a second. Who's this?" She held the earphones to Harley and leaned close so they could both listen.

"That's Vicky," he said.

"A confrontation is not a great idea at this point," Robbins said.

"Tell *her*."

Robbins shook her head helplessly. "This is why we need to make contact."

"Can't we just . . ." Harley didn't even know what the options were.

"Storm the place?" Robbins answered. "That's one option. Swing someone in from the floor above, through the broken window. Create a diversion. Cut the power so all the lights go off—our guys will have incautious about how they go in. Because in that case there are—ta da—innocent victims, and they don't want to make the situation worse. Same here. Plus, this woman is in there giving birth."

"All the more reason to get in and get out and get her some medical attention," Harley said. "Which is why she came to the hospital in the first place."

"All right, but it's like there are two separate crises going on. On the one hand, childbirth. Not that these guys are wimps or anything. I'd be willing to bet that someone on that squad has delivered a baby in a crisis situation. Police do that, you know."

"Yeah."

"But they'd rather not upset that balance. At least this is my guess. And the other crisis is the suspect. Now, if the woman would just deliver that baby, as they've been expecting she would any minute for the past hour, that would be one crisis they wouldn't have to solve. So they could just go for the madman."

Harley remembered his mother, who'd expected updates every five minutes or so when Beebe was in labor, and how he'd kept holding off, thinking any minute he would have some real news.

"Anyway, hostage situations are different. Usually, patience is the key. The suspect probably doesn't have a lot but we've got plenty. That's our weapon. Time."

Harley wondered how much all these folks were costing the police department. Surely there was some overtime. Or maybe they were just doing their normal job that they'd be paid for anyway. "I guess I figured they'd go right in," he said. "There are a lot of them, right?"

"On the squad? Maybe six or eight," Robbins said. "I really don't know."

"Guess I'm in some trouble, huh?" He caresses the gun again.

"Yeah." I'm in some trouble too. We all are. "But you got here all by yourself, didn't you? Now, how do you think you're gonna get out?" If he pointed the gun at his face and fired I wouldn't care.

He doesn't. Nor does he answer. I reach out and slowly put my hand around the wrist holding the gun, a touch he could shake off very easily. "We could just walk out. We could get out of here now, and let these people have their baby in peace, after all this. Come on." He doesn't move. I know I have a tendency to say too much, so I shut up. I stare into his eyes, trying to will him to do what I asked, to follow me, to respond to the gentle pressure on his wrist. In the dim light his eyes are very dark.

Behind us, I hear the nurse urging Deanna to give it all she has, this is it, push! At least a minute goes by, and then Deanna gasps, "Oh, oh, oh."

Lookabaugh lowers the hand holding the gun, and my hand along with it. Without losing eye contact I release his wrist and hold both hands up in front of me, a shield to keep him from going back in there. A pretty pathetic shield, if you want to know the truth. But for the moment that's my job, keeping him out of there. That was my job all along, and I failed.

He doesn't seem to need a shield. He drops into the chair. His eyes glisten in the dark.

Then I hear the tiny voice, not really crying, almost mimicking Deanna's, only saying "aa, aa, aa."

"Pant, don't push for a minute. Okay, one more. Okay! Here he is!" Now there was a pro. Arden de-

these moods. But he wouldn't really hurt anybody. "He's—you know—he can be sorta bossy," she said, talking considerably slower than she had earlier in the evening. "Wants his own way. Like, he'll do things, he'll smash stuff, if one of the boys doesn't mind him he might, like, tear up their bicycle, or once he, well, Stevie did something naughty, and he pulled all the patches off his Cub Scout shirt, but he would never spank them or anything—"

"Psychological torture," Robbins muttered to Harley. "*So* much more effective when paired with physical abuse, but fairly effective on its own."

"Or, like, he'd decide that somebody was kind of, you know, in the doghouse, and that nobody else in the family should speak to him for a while, that kind of thing, like time out, or go to your room, only see, nobody had their own room—"

"So why'd he bring a gun?" Swartz demanded.

Barb crossed her leg and shifted her chair away from him an inch or so. "That's a new thing, I mean, a new one, I mean, not a new gun, but, not something he's ever done before. But I don't even know, in fact I doubt that they're loaded—"

"He's *fired* them," Swartz said.

Barb swallowed and shifted her chair back another quarter inch. "Did he—hit anyone?"

Swartz stared at her. "He could have."

"He's never done that before. It's just another way to get what he wants. But he's never hurt anybody!"

"So what does he want?" Chopak asked gently.

"I don't know!" Barb said. "You know he sued the hospital, and what he said he wanted was his wife—me—made whole, but that's just nuts." She shook her

The well-dressed psychopath needs such an accessory.

Does he always carry a starched white handkerchief around, or only when he plans to go out and commit mayhem? Maybe he planned for tears. Anyway I would have figured him as a bandanna type.

For the first time since I ran into him, he isn't holding either of his guns. Probably, at this moment, Deanna, Alexi, and Arden could march out of the room. I beam them a message to do so.

I don't know if Deanna could manage it. The typical procedure here is to offer what we call a "walking epidural." A lot of mothers think that means they can still walk around while under its influence. They can't. They can move their legs, but they'd need assistance to walk around—and the epidural is attached, along with a blood pressure monitor on a separate stand, along with, usually, another IV pole. Quite a lot of equipment to tote around behind you, in other words.

Deanna's epidural has worn off enough for her to feel the delivery—that was pretty obvious. But she's just given birth. Back when I was still a nurse, a woman who'd given birth only fifteen minutes before walked down six flights of stairs during an emergency evacuation, so it can be done. And this is definitely an emergency.

At any rate, whether Deanna can walk or not, those folks aren't picking up on my silent message at all. Guess none of them are psychic. Too bad. As Plan B, maybe I could get Peter out. In fact, that seems better all around.

I reach out to him again.

This time, when I touch his wrist, I have an instant

of here without his cooperation. Even given that he's not a particularly large man.

I host a brief pity party of my own. *Anybody* could drag him out of there, except me. Harley, for instance. Or Father Gifford, an extremely large guy and our head chaplain—he would simply pick Lookabaugh up and haul him out, possibly even if Peter still had a gun in his hand. And one of them would have had to do it, too, if only I hadn't answered my goddamned phone.

"Come on, Peter, that's beside the point," I say. "I don't believe everyone hates you. Your children. They don't hate you. And Barb." I try desperately, and hopelessly, to think of other people who might not hate him. He could very well be right.

Then I figure he picked up on my hostility, you might call it, when I touched him, somehow. Obviously he's either very sensitive to body language, or psychic. I try transferring my hostility elsewhere. To my cell phone. If I ever get out of here—strike that, *when* I get out of here—I'm going to throw it into the fountain. No, that's too good for it. First I'll throw it out the window, with a lot of force. Then I'll go down and stomp on it a few times, *then* I'll throw it into the fountain.

"They'll shoot me if I go out that door," he says.

He might be right about that too. I certainly hope so. But no, I have to think happy thoughts, or at least neutral ones. "I'll go out first," I say. "If anybody's out there," and I devoutly hope somebody is, "they'll expect you to come out with a hostage and they'll hold their fire. But I haven't heard anybody out there."

I pull gently on his wrist and take half a step backward toward the door. He takes my other hand—he's

through the gap between the curtain and the wall, Deanna sitting up, learning how to nurse her baby, and Alexi looking nervously in our direction. I can't see the nurse, but I don't dare shift my gaze.

"Peter—"

"I've got unfinished business. Getting out of here won't get me any closer to that doctor. No—I think she's gonna have to come to me."

"Peter . . ." I can't think of anything to say to get him out of here. I can't drag him out. I can't even keep him aimed toward the door.

Moments before I had been ready to fling the door open and drop to the floor to give a clear shot at Peter Lookabaugh. Now I'm ready to fall to the floor and pound my fists on it. Except then I'd have to let his hands go, and he'd pick the guns up again. I guess I made some progress after all.

The nurse ignores both of us and goes to the sink. For a minute I stare into the gun. I know it's a small gun but it looks enormous. And so close. Couldn't possibly miss me. Then I hear water running. I remember the nurse's name is Arden, not Arlys. She fills the plastic pitcher then steps behind us—not as close as before—back behind the curtain and urges Deanna to drink up.

My knees are weak, but I seem to be too tired to be really pissed off. Which is too bad. When I yelled at Lookabaugh it seemed to take him by surprise, which is what I need to do again, to get him out of here. Now that Arden mentioned it, I'm thirsty. Oh, and I have a headache. And my feet hurt.

Peter Lookabaugh is still pointing the gun at me. Well, he's been doing that all night and he hasn't shot me yet. But this constant gun-waving is getting annoying.

"Water," I say. "Good idea." I walk around Lookabaugh, ignoring the gun as Arden did, and go to the sink, where of course there are no glasses. I turn the faucet on and stick my head under it. It isn't that cold, I don't like drinking out of a faucet, and I don't like tap water in any case, but it refreshes me. I'm still too tired to get mad.

From the other side of the curtain Arden says, "This gal could use some nourishment, too."

"Too bad we don't have a phone," I mutter. "We could call out for a pizza." For some reason Lookabaugh finds this funny and laughs.

"There's sandwiches in the fridge at the nurses' station," Arden says. "We keep them for the new mothers. They always seem to deliver after the kitchen's closed and they're always hungry."

"Sure you will," he says to the curtain. "Or I'll start shooting people again. How long you think it'll take you? Two minutes?"

"It's on the other side of the floor," Arden says. "But I'm not going if you make threats about me not coming back. I don't want that burden. This young lady needs rest and peace more than she needs food, and sounds like my leaving will break the peace. Such as it is."

After a long moment of silence, Lookabaugh says, "Okay, well, I have a candy bar in my pocket. She can have that." He digs around for a moment and actually comes up with half a Snickers, with the wrapper folded around it. It looks completely unappetizing, yet it makes me drool.

He hands it to me. I swallow and hand it around the curtain to Arden.

"I'll go get the sandwiches," Arden says. "But only if there's no shooting. No threats. I'll get one for everybody."

I don't think that will sell Peter. Not only does he not look hungry, he just gave away a candy bar. But he surprises me. "Okay," he says. Then he shoves the curtain to one side again.

The light over the bed seemed so impossibly dim when Arden first turned it on. Now it seems bright. In the moments while my eyes adjust to the brighter light, Arden quickly drops a sheet over Deanna's legs. Deanna herself reclines, eyes closed, tightly holding a red-faced but peaceful infant. Arden rearranges her pillows. Alexi glares at Peter Lookabaugh. You wouldn't need a lot of light to read that glare.

Arden moves in front of Alexi and tucks the sheet in

opens her eyes. Lookabaugh speaks first. "I knew they were out there. How many are there?"

Alexi stares at the floor. "I don't know," he says. "I think there were two of them that grabbed me. More behind them. A bunch."

I feel a grim little smile trying to take over my lips. I squelch it.

"They have guns?" Lookabaugh asks.

"Don't be an idiot," I snap. "Of course they have guns. You said so yourself. What did you think they were going to shoot you with, water pistols?"

Deanna's blue eyes widen as she looks at me, then at Lookabaugh.

He only laughs again. I'm beginning to hate the sound of that laugh.

"She isn't coming back," Lookabaugh says after a minute. "You were right, Miss Vicky. We need a phone."

"Too bad you shot the only one in the room."

"Maybe we can get it to work."

Fat chance. I remember pieces of hot plastic flying all over. The metal guts of the phone, with the receiver attached, are still on the floor next to the wall, where somebody kicked them out of the way of the bed.

Lookabaugh kneels down and picks up the receiver, listens, and jiggles a few of the mangled pieces. That phone couldn't possibly work, ever again.

"There's other rooms," he says confidently. "Right? Phone in every room. And as far as I can tell, most of these rooms are empty."

My mind leaps ahead, visualizing Lookabaugh leaving in search of a phone. In other words, a leap into

Alexi glances at Deanna and the baby, then back at Peter. "I guess that's okay," he says. "I mean, yeah, we can do that, sure."

"You take the baby," Lookabaugh says.

Alexi balks. "We leave the baby out. We leave the baby with Deanna, here."

"Nope," Lookabaugh says coolly. "Baby's part of the deal."

Alexi looks anguished for half a second, then he explodes. "Hey, no way! This whole thing's about you not getting a baby, right? Only I heard you say you had eight. How come you get eight and we don't even get one? You can kill me, man, you're not getting my baby."

"Just a minute," I say.

"Never mind, it was a bad idea," Lookabaugh interrupts. "We don't need to go parading down the hall. I have another idea. We'll just go get another phone."

"Splendid idea," I mutter.

"You said these rooms are all alike, and they all have phones—right?"

"Right."

"You," Lookabaugh says, pointing the gun at Alexi. "Come over here."

Alexi complies, slowly. Deanna opens her eyes, then shuts them tight.

"No, it's okay, I won't shoot him if he does what I say," Peter says soothingly. "I just need him for a minute. And you, Miss Vicky." He switches the gun to me. "We're going over to the door for a minute. Miss Vicky's going to nab us a phone from another room."

He herds Alexi and me to the door, then grabs Alexi and holds the gun to his neck. "Okay, Miss Vicky, open the door."

even though I don't think he can see me. Then I dial zero.

"Arden Stonecipher?" The woman, small and dark, nodded to Phil Swartz. "You related to Gunner Stonecipher? The CU quarterback?"

"Theodore, his name is," Arden said. "My son. I don't much like that nickname."

"It's the way he fires that ball," Swartz said.

"I know that. I still don't like it. Can I sit down?"

"Sure, sit . . ." Swartz looked her over. Composed, small, dark, and very calm. Some kind of inner peace. Maybe she was a Hindu? A Buddhist? Her son was 6′4″, weighed 240, curly-haired, handsome, and some kind of hell-raiser both on and off the field. But that was in Boulder. "Tell me about what's going on in there."

"That man, Lookabaugh, does not know guns," she said. "He can shoot them, but he does it all wrong. He just kind of points them and fires. Doesn't sight. Doesn't hold them properly. Doesn't really aim, everything he's hit, he's been close to. Yanks on the trigger. Not that he couldn't kill somebody."

She sounded like somebody who knew her own way around guns.

"You have any idea what kind of gun? And whether he can reload it?"

She eased back into the chair and shut her eyes for a minute. "I really don't know that much about guns myself. A semiautomatic, black, with a metal magazine, about like so." She positioned her hands about six inches apart. "And a shotgun."

"You didn't see him reload?"

She shook her head. "I don't think he wants to kill

previous nurse. See, I haven't even worked my full shift. Feels like it, though."

"Anything else you can tell us that might be helpful?"

"I don't know if it's helpful, but there's a hypo of Nubain under Deanna's pillow. I was going to stick it in that man, if the opportunity presented itself, but it never did."

"What would it do?" Swartz asked.

"It's a sedative. . . . I don't know if it would knock him out, but it would slow him down, and it does work fast."

"It wouldn't just make him mad?" Chopak wondered. "If he's nuts, you know, sometimes drugs don't have an effect."

The nurse turned toward Chopak. "That's true. But it was the only thing I could think of. And, you see, I never got to find out. I just thought it might be helpful if somebody in that room knew it was there."

"Okay, good," Swartz said. "You did a great job in there, under a lot of pressure."

Arden pursed her lips. "How do you know that?"

"Oh, uh—" Before Swartz could tell her they had a transmitter on Alexi, Chopak interrupted him. "Because you got out."

"Answer!" I scream at the phone in a whisper. "Come on, dammit, pick up the fucking phone, somebody!" Dialing zero should have connected me to the hospital switchboard, and somebody should have picked up within three rings. I had convinced myself that help and salvation lay at the other end of the line. I never like to admit I'm wrong.

rate it's nice to be out of Lookabaugh's gaze. A little solitude.

I study the phone. I don't really want to cut the cable, partly because I'm afraid then we'd never get it back together, and partly because I'm afraid to cut into electrical-looking things for fear of being electrocuted. I do know cutting through an ordinary phone wire wouldn't hurt you—once I accidentally cut one with a three-hole punch—but these are complicated things, hooked into all sorts of buzzers and lights.

I set the phone on the bed and study it while I dial Harley's extension. A breathless female voice answers "Yes?" even before I can pry the little screwdriver out of the Swiss army knife.

"This is Vicky Lucci," I whisper into the phone. "I am on the fourth floor—"

"I know who you are," she whispers back, then speaks in a regular voice. "Hold tight. You have a phone in that room? We've had people trying to call."

A quick study. "I'm in another room, unscrewing the phone at this moment, to take back into room 4426."

"Good," she says. "Just a minute." I hear her tell somebody she has a hostage on the line. Damn it, *I'm still a hostage*. I keep twirling the screwdriver. Lucky thing I spend half my life with a phone clamped to my shoulder. I'm in top form for using both hands to take a phone apart while talking on it.

A lower, huskier female voice speaks next. "We have you surrounded. If you can get the suspect in front of the window and singled out we might be able to get a shot off."

The immediate appeal of this idea quickly gives way

member where these wires go. When I take it back in the other room I mean."

"Oh shit," the woman says. "We really need to be in contact with the suspect."

"You said it, sister," I mutter. Louder, I announce, "I think I'm going to need to write this down or something. It's complicated." I lay the phone gently on the bed, stand up, note that I feel kind of dizzy, and go to the door.

"There's got to be paper in here somewhere." I expect Peter to pull some out of his pocket. Maybe turn it into a paper airplane and sail it down the hall to me. Instead he throws me a felt-tip pen.

No problem. I can work with that. I have, golly gee, toilet paper and paper towels to choose from. No, I can be more creative than that. I rip an obstetrical pad—essentially, a foot-long sanitary napkin—out of its wrapper and use the wrapper.

"Okay," I say, for Lookabaugh's benefit. "I'm writing this down now. Give me a minute."

The woman on the other end says, "First, and probably most important, don't be a hero. Now. Two principles. One, keep him talking, let him talk as much as he wants. Try to be sympathetic. Make him feel like you're on his side." Yes. That was my own idea, hours ago, or essentially my idea: listen to him. Let him vent. "The other thing is, make us the bad guys. Try to forge a connection. Among you, I mean."

"Got it." In fact, I almost wrote it down.

"And about those sandwiches, I've been overruled. You can get them."

"All right!"

12

"Here's how it will go," I say. "I'll walk down that hall. You'll be able to see me all the way to the end. Then, just as it turns, that's where the nurses' station is."

"Where we were earlier," Lookabaugh says.

"Right." It seems like days ago. "I'll be in there maybe a minute. Maybe less. Then I'll come out, and you'll be able to see me all the way back."

"I still don't think they'll let you come back."

I shrug. "Okay, well, we've got the phone anyway."

"Ah, hell," Lookabaugh says. "Give it a try."

"Right." I hand him the phone, noting that he'll have to let go of Alexi in order to take it. He does. I think about trying to palm the Swiss army knife, because you never know. I'd slip it into my pocket if I had a pocket, but I don't. I also don't have a good grasp on it and don't want to look like I'm hanging on to it, so Lookabaugh gets that back, too. What the hell. The only thing I can do with a knife is cut my steak.

"You have to talk to me all the way," he says, setting the phone on the floor and kicking it inside. "I don't hear your voice, then . . ." he draws his forefinger across his neck.

marry him, they both said yes, he decided he didn't want either one of them, and this prompted him to want to get far away. Mostly, far away from their fathers. This may have been the same kind of trouble that made a name change and flight from Lithuania seem like a good idea. And also he had not been diligent in saving money to get the rest of his family over here. But what the hell.

"Yeah," I say, talking louder now because I'm farther away. "That was pretty much it. He was an outlaw, but a pretty mild one."

"Tell me what he did!"

I try to think of something dastardly, something that would still carry weight more than a hundred years later. I fail. "He got engaged to two girls at the same time. So he came West and changed his name, only he didn't change it too much. From Lacchi."

Damn it, what's wrong with me? I could have said he was running from the law and had long-standing Sicilian connections, which are still in place. Insinuated that these vengeance-oriented Italians could be coming after Lookabaugh if he does anything bad to me.

I pass the elevators and note that the exit light is off, a light that should never go off, even in the case of a power failure. I conscientiously don't look into the well of darkness as I pass, in case the sharpshooters are hanging out there. That's where they'd be. Lookabaugh prompts me to keep talking. "So, like, he couldn't spell? Or he couldn't spell in English?"

"As far as I know he wasn't real educated."

"But they never caught up with him, right? He didn't come to a bad end or anything?"

some scrubs and getting out of my light silk dress. Which is probably ruined, all things considered. At least I didn't have to catch the baby. That can really mess up an outfit.

"What are you doing?" Lookabaugh bellows.

"I'm—"

—grabbed by a man in black. Well, not grabbed. He touches my arm and holds a finger to his mouth, which is not a mouth but a mask. I ignore the gesture.

"I'm looking for sandwiches!"

"Keep talking!"

The guy in black nods. "Right!" To the guy in black I say, "I have to go back." Then I yell, "It's a dumb name, Lucci, I know that, and people do occasionally mispronounce it. Look-Eye. Lusky. Loose-Eye, Look-See. But about half of all the people who try it get it right!"

To the guy in black I whisper, "He's standing in the doorway with one of the hostages. The husband of the patient. Supposedly, he'll shoot him if I don't go back."

"My great-uncle rode for the Pony Express!" I yell for Lookabaugh's benefit. And where did he get his name, I'd like to know? I'll have to ask him.

"They know you're here," I say to the guy in black, who nods again. "Alexi let it out that there were people out here who didn't want to let him come back."

"Everybody says that!" Lookabaugh bellows. "It's like Woodstock. Everybody says they were at Woodstock, everybody! Everybody had an uncle in the Pony Express! Everybody's a Navy SEAL!"

"This is fucking *nuts*," I mutter to my escort in black as I open the refrigerator. It smells like any office refrigerator, a little in need of cleaning. The new moms' sand-

Lookabaugh, "I'm coming out now." I hesitate, giving the guy in black a chance to stick his head out and maybe take a shot at Lookabaugh. I am very disappointed when he chooses not to do so.

Damn it, why doesn't somebody *save me*? They've had chances and chances. I am done in. My feet hurt. I'm cold. I never got a chance to look for scrubs. I stink and my eyelids are drooping. I try to think how things could be worse. Well, I could be staked to an anthill somewhere. I could be bleeding to death. Resentfully, I slip out, leaving the green glow and the buzz, and walk down the dark hall to where Peter Lookabaugh waits.

One of the juice jugs slips out of my grasp. "Can you grab that?" I entreat. And he tucks the gun somewhere and grabs it.

Hey, I'm good at this bonding stuff. Here we are, working together as a team.

Lookabaugh lets Alexi go and we all move inside and shut the door.

Even with fresh air flowing through the broken window the room smells close. Sort of like a stable in winter. Actually, cozy, in a strange kind of way, the way a bed smells when you've got the flu and have been nesting in it and sweating and having weird dreams. After a minute, I find it hard to believe I was out of the room at all.

I dump the sandwiches on the counter and pour the juice into Deanna's glass, the only glass in the room. The rest of us will just have to swig it out of the carton.

"You really need to hit the liquids," I tell her. "Drink up. What kind of sandwich do you want?"

"Any kind," she says faintly, cuddling the baby in her arm. A good baby. Sleeping.

ing on. "It's fair. It's the Lord's will," he says. " 'I will greatly multiply your sorrow and your conception. In pain ye shall bring forth children.' It's in Genesis, right after they get kicked out of the Garden of Eden. On account of eating the fruit of the tree of knowledge. It's part of the punishment."

So much for lightening the mood. The smell of the room returns, overpowering the sandwich. The tasty turkey and crisp lettuce in my mouth turn into dead flesh and some kind of chewy, tasteless weed—although I keep chewing. Thank you, Captain Bringdown. I shouldn't have said anything about babies at all. So I keep my response to myself, that response being that in actual fact a human baby's brain is about a hundred times bigger than the polar bear's will *ever* get.

We munch away in gloomy silence. I consider some pretext to get Peter to the window. If nobody shoots him I could give him a shove.

He doesn't even need my diagram. He's using his head—finding the wire on the old, shot-up phone, removing it, and placing it directly in the corresponding spot on the new phone.

Then I remember the Last Word, a silly little device that one of our administrators brought into the office. It was the size and shape of a pager, with a button on the side. But when you pushed the button, it said, in an electronically generated voice, gender-neutral but slightly on the high side: "Eat shit!" If you pressed it again, it said, "Fuck you!" One more time and it came out with, "You're an asshole!" Those three phrases were its entire repertoire.

For some reason—probably our complete lack of taste or sensitivity—all of us in Admin. found this in-their hands. Especially in light of all the recent bad publicity. Gives them confidence.

Deanna is finished with her sandwich, too. I shield her from Lookabaugh with my body and once again check her skin elasticity, which could be better. "Drink up," I tell her. "Water, juice, everything. You really need these liquids."

She gazes at me with wide blue eyes. "Because of the breastfeeding?"

"That too. But mainly to keep up your energy, your electrolytes, to help replace all the fluids you've lost." Speaking of which, I check her again. The lighting is dim and the bleeding is profuse, but then it always is. Deliveries are unbelievably bloody. Awkwardly I change her pad again, then even more awkwardly replace her stained Chux liner with a new one. As I do, I wonder if a genuine medical emergency would soften Lookabaugh's heart—it would probably freak Deanna and Alexi out for a minute but it would be worth it, if it worked—

—and immediately reject this idea. Deanna was in a medical emergency when we came in, and Lookabaugh used it to try to get Dr. Hawthorne in here. He'd do it again. I pull the sheet over Deanna and urge her once again to drink up and then, as I start to back away, Lookabaugh seizes my arm.

"Okay," he says. "The phone's working. We're gonna get that doctor up here, now." And he hauls me a few steps backward to the phone.

When he lets go, I rub my arm. Try to say something nonconfrontational.

"You got it together already?"

"How serious do you think this is?" I catch something in her voice.

"Oh, it's serious. Um, I don't have a lot of experience in postpartum but there is a lot of blood and the patient is . . . faint." This is not a lie.

"Put the sus—Mr. Lookabaugh on the phone," Chopak orders.

I thrust the receiver at Peter. "Here. She wants to talk to you."

He takes the receiver, stares at it, finally holds it up to his ear. Yeah, Peter, a phone. "The doctor?" he says.

I don't answer. Let him find out for himself.

Harley watched silently as Chopak threw Swartz a thumbs-up sign.

"Contact," Robbins whispered to Harley. "Now all we have to do is be quiet while she handles it."

"We can't do that without a guarantee of the doctor's safety," Chopak said into the phone. "And furthermore, I don't believe the doctor you requested is available now. We would be happy to send a doctor, but we need a show of good faith on your part first, and so far there hasn't been any."

Harley heard Lookabaugh's reply, barely, through the earphone. Something about how he took no responsibility for the patient's condition if a doctor wasn't summoned immediately. Of course, Harley'd been listening all along, so he knew it was a set up; he also knew that, in fact, the patient probably *did* need medical attention. Well, there was a vast spectrum of need.

"I understand all that," Chopak said. "Also that the patient is in this dire situation solely because of your actions this evening. I think we all understand that, too.

"Okay," Lookabaugh says. "Sure. I'll talk to Barb." Another minute passes and then, inexplicably, he hands the receiver back to me.

I sure as hell don't want to talk to Barb. But I take it.

It's Swartz, speaking in a somewhat lower voice than before. "We're preparing his wife to talk to him. Someone will be listening in, of course. What we told you before, that still goes."

"Uh huh." My mind whirls. I should have written it down on the back of my hand. Don't be a hero. Keep him talking. Make them the bad guys. "Is there a plan?"

"We've got resources," Swartz says. "His wife is here, and she's being coached by a psychologist, actually a psychiatric social worker, who specializes in hostage situations. I cannot overemphasize that you are not to do anything impulsive. We have a perfect record in regard to hostage safety. In addition to the psychiatrist we've got your chaplain and the family's priest standing by."

"Sounds like some kind of joke."

"Excuse me?"

"You know. A shrink, a chaplain, a priest, and a cop walk into a hospital, and so forth." Oh shit, did I just do something impulsive? I hope I haven't blown the game plan by revealing this to Lookabaugh. But I think not. In fact I think I should have said "a SWAT team" instead of "a cop."

"Oh. I see. Lightening the tension. Heh-heh." The guy apparently has no sense of humor. That was a nonlaugh if ever I heard one. "Well, I think she's ready. You can give the phone back to him now."

I wish I could tell this guy that what he probably wants is Lookabaugh's mother-in-law on that phone.

pushed together. Barb picked up the phone and held it to her ear, looking like a scared rabbit. The shrink sat down beside her. "Talk slowly," he said.

"You can tell him we found his truck in the parking lot," Swartz said. "Ask him what he thought he was doing with that explosive stuff."

Barb took a deep breath.

"Okay," Swartz said. "You're on."

She leaned forward. "Hello. Honey? Peter?" Then she paused. Even Gifford opened his eyes.

"No, it's me. Honest. I'm here in the hospital. Really. Oh, over where we used to meet, you know . . ." She stopped and stared at Swartz and seemed to be making every effort to speak slowly. "Really. Um, they found your truck. . . . Yes, honey, it's me, it's really me. . . ." She held the phone out from her ear.

"He doesn't believe it's me," she stage-whispered to Swartz. And then added, "But really I think he knows it is."

Harley figured speaking slowly was such a strain on her that Peter Lookabaugh didn't recognize her voice.

"Keep talking," Swartz said.

"But he hung up!" Barb looked baffled.

From the other desk, Chopak held up a finger. "She's right. He broke the connection."

"Should I call him back?" Barb asked.

"No!" Chopak said. "He initiated the contact, and he'll have to initiate the next one, too. And I believe he will."

"Clarify," her partner Swartz said. "Why aren't we attempting to get the doctor, get her in here, and get her on the phone?"

"Or, what did he say? It could be an attaché, a gym bag, a backpack? Any of those things?"

"I don't know what you're talking about."

Swartz motioned to Robbins, who came to his side. Chopak did something to her lips that made her look like a frog who'd just caught a fly.

Swartz whispered to Robbins, and Robbins came over to Harley and spoke to him in a low voice. "You remember when Alexi went back in. Did you hear that?"

Harley shook his head and watched Barb.

"We can't figure out if Barb heard that or if she knows something," Robbins said.

"I don't think she did," Harley said. "How could she? But somebody might have said something. What, you didn't have somebody looking for a bag? Satchel, or whatever?"

Robbins shook her head and turned her attention back to Swartz.

"You need to level with us," he said to Barb. "How much of a threat is your husband and what would stop him?"

Barb shut her mouth. But not for long. "I don't know," she said. "He's never been like this. I mean he was always stubborn, and stuff, but this, it's like he's just lost his mind. Like he's just lost his mind." She bit her lip. "In the spring he got fired from his coaching job—this wasn't a job for pay, just coaching Petey's baseball team—that's our eight-year-old, well no, he turned nine—because he yelled at the kids, *all* of them, and they aren't supposed to yell, even when they do stupid stuff that makes them lose the game."

"So," Chopak said. "Would you say his self-control is disintegrating?"

"Uh, no," Barb said. She looked from Chopak to the psychiatrist.

"What we're getting at," he said deliberately, "is sometimes, actually more often than you'd think, somebody will sort of set themself up, so that the police have no choice, really, except to shoot them."

Barb shut her eyes, then rubbed her temples. She started talking before she opened her eyes again. "Well he might do something like that, might think about it. I mean he's been under the weather lately, his aunt died, they were pretty close, well at one time they were, she wasn't all that old, and then. . . . actually you know we got the call, that she was in the hospital and all, during Matt's graduation party, we were all out in the backyard and drinking beer, just the adults I mean, drinking, that is, and the phone rang and it was his uncle, who he doesn't like all that much, well the guy is pretty much a jerk, but fortunately I picked up the phone and—"

Chopak's sharp voice stopped her. "Mrs. Lookabaugh!"

Barb wound down. "Anyway we had to decide, you know, whether to tell people at the party, we didn't want to ruin Matt's day. But anyway. She died." She took a breath. Chopak jumped in.

"Sometimes the death of a close relative can cause this kind of reaction. Usually it's someone closer, a parent, but was he pretty close to this aunt?"

"Oh yes, in fact he lived with her, that is, she raised him. After his mother died and he didn't get along with his stepfather."

"So it could have been a pretty close relationship, almost parental."

Barb screwed her eyes shut. "He *liked* his aunt but I

Harley raised his eyebrows. "And if she wants to?"

"She'll have to be discouraged."

"That wasn't her," Peter says. "They're mousetrapping me."

"They probably are," I agree. "But that was probably her, all the same. I mean, she's here, Peter. I saw her."

I rub the area around my eyes. I have on bulletproof mascara, the kind of stuff you need a special solvent to get off, so I'm not worried about smearing it, but my eyes feel grainy. I have been wearing my extended-wear contact lenses for an extended period, and my vision's blurry. My eye doctor said not to sleep in them. No problem there. I haven't slept.

"I *know* my wife's voice," Lookabaugh growls.

I try to imagine a conversation between the Lookabaughs. I never actually heard them have one. Typically, when I met with them, Barb arrived first and poured out her heart and soul nonstop until Peter showed up. He was always late. They always came from two different places, having deposited various children in various other places. When he walked in the door, Barb would say, "Oh, *hi*, honey," as if seeing him were a big surprise, and then she didn't say another word except in response to a direct question. Even in those cases she let him answer if at all possible.

Maybe he doesn't let her talk at all, and that's why the words flow out of her whenever he's not present. At first, I just figured it was the only chance she had for an adult conversation. Not that you could call it a conversation.

it will help." I wish I hadn't let the thought of serious complications into my head.

I probe Deanna's neck, checking for swollen lymph nodes as well as fever. I wince when I hear a click behind me and turn to look. Peter has the TV remote, which I guess was on the floor somewhere. He's turned the TV on, again with no sound.

Well, good. Maybe it will distract him.

No swelling in the lymph nodes, but Deanna's temp is definitely elevated, and this concerns me. It's not unusual for women to develop a slight fever following childbirth, but it's also something you report to the doctor. Right away. Of the thousands of women who've died in childbirth over the course of the last million years, a large percentage were done in by infections.

I cover her up again and look around the room, without even realizing at first what I'm looking for. Oh yeah. My purse. With my pharmacopeia. Even given that in recent years my once bountiful drug supply has shrunk, I would still have the basics: ibuprofen, Midol, antihistamines of one sort or another that could be useful to bump Deanna over the edge into sleep. Would that be a good idea? I might even have some old antibiotics rattling around. But—*shit!*—I hadn't carried my usual large bag tonight, just an evening purse. A thing so inconsequential that I didn't even bring it along when I so brazenly marched down the hall to check L&D for bogeymen. I thought I'd be right back.

Ah, hell. Just as well. Deanna could be allergic to something. With any luck she's not, and her chart will tell me, assuming I still know how to read a chart. It's hanging from a hook behind the head of the bed.

14

It only lasts for a minute, but it's another one of those *long* minutes. There *I* am, surrounded by drunken friends, freshly lipsticked, wearing the dress I'm still wearing.

Peter looks from me to the TV and back again. "Wow," he says, as if this is the most exciting thing that's happened to him all night.

I blink. Is this really happening? And then the camera cuts to another freshly lipsticked woman, live, at the Medallion. I know it's live because it says so in one corner of the screen. I know what she's probably saying, too, that Montmorency Medical Center is the scene of a hostage situation, blah blah blah. I even know where she got the picture.

Sassy.

I wonder how much the all-night news crew paid Sassy for this Polaroid. I wonder how much information Sassy gave them. Do the media know, for instance, that I was pulled away from a night of revelry to be taken hostage by some lunkhead with an ax to grind? For some reason this picture embarrasses me deeply.

Then I wonder if they are *all* here, in the limo, if the scene at the hospital has become part of the festivities.

big family, for one thing—not quite as big as Look-abaugh's but with endless sets of cousins, who are everywhere—and they are all athletic and have good teeth. It's easy enough to imagine them all out playing touch football at the compound. Only, they don't. They play polo.

Lookabaugh is as riveted to the screen as he would be if he could hear what the newswoman is saying.

I stand by Deanna's bed, kind of swaying on my feet and thinking about all the things in my nice big purse that would be handy to have. Then I remember that I was carrying an evening bag instead of my nice big purse. But I still had the essentials. Eye drops and contact lens case, lipstick, cell phone, cigarettes, breath mints, perfume. Things that could give me comfort, nothing that could get me out of this goddamned room. Outside, I hear the birds twittering.

Stupid birds. Why do they get up so goddamn early, anyway? What's the point? Oh—right, the worm.

I have to get out of here. "Peter," I say, "You wanna be on TV? We could call up. I'll bet we could get you on there."

He jerks his head. "Naw. I just want that doctor."

I try to mask my annoyance with him but probably don't, because his next words are, "Yeah. Same old thing I've always been asking for."

Why hide it? "Peter," I say impatiently, "you talked to the doctor. In fact you talked and talked and *talked* to the doctor. And every time you talked to the doctor, it seemed to me like what she said made sense. I mean, it seemed to me like it made sense to you—"

"I know what you mean!"

"I mean, how did it affect you? How did it affect Barb?"

Now I have his full attention. "Hey, we lost a baby."

"I know. I'm sorry." I can't think of anything else to say. I sort of lost sight of that. They had, indeed, lost a baby.

"Okay," he says, facing me. "It's not just the baby. I mean that was hard and all, particularly on Barb. She thought kids needed brothers and sisters. She only had this brother, way older than her, and he went off to join the Air Force when she was like, six. He didn't even seem like a brother to her, except that her parents talked about him a lot. Which they did because he went missing in action and nobody knew for about ten years what had even happened to him. She wanted a family, one that lasted. See, her father turned into a crazy man, I mean really crazy . . . after we moved into the house, he was living in a trailer, an RV, back behind the barn, and he was, like, gone. You know, dingy." Peter twirls his forefinger at his temple in the universal symbol for crazy. "Yeah, you think I'm some kind of nut but lemme tell you, you ain't seen nothing, Miss Vicky. He lived there on beans and Old Crow and never came out. *But . . .*"

Peter pauses significantly. I wait.

"But, every time we took that trip to the hospital, and we'd come back with a little bundle of joy, we'd go and knock on his door, and he'd come in and give us this grin. Lost all his teeth, he did, but he'd grin, and then he'd clean up for a while and be a grandpa."

"So she did it, kept having all those kids, for her father?"

shriek these words that Deanna was actually drifting into sleep, but not anymore. "What do you want?"

Peter Lookabaugh looks frightened, but it's probably just some kind of act. I can't figure him out at all. Neither one of them.

"I'm just trying for a little parity!" he yells back. "That's all, okay? Just a little of some kind of thing called life. Hospital fucks you over, you get something for it. That's all!"

"You got something. I wrote off the bill. The *entire* bill, for the miscarriage, the surgery, everything. Dr. Hawthorne wrote off *her* bill."

"But it shouldn't have even happened! We shouldn't have gotten a bill for that. Why should we? It wasn't our fault."

Ah, Jesus. "It wasn't our fault either. And we still had to pay the staff. We still had expenses. You know, you're a farmer, right? You have a bad year. You still have to pay for your seed and fertilizer and you've still put in the time."

"And I don't get paid for that! You got it, it's a write-off. But we're talking about some fucking carnations and tomatoes and stuff, and what I'm talking about is a human life!"

Arrgh! I've had conversations like this before. With Lookabaugh before, even, but with others as well. It's one of the problems of being a lawyer. You don't know everything, but you're a reasonable person, such as is mentioned in all the legal textbooks, so people hire you to point out the reason to other people, and it seems easy enough. Except the other people aren't reasonable people. Only they think *they* are reasonable and you aren't. Or something.

when things get good, if they ever do, then something happens."

"Yeah—"

"Everything goes sour. But some people have it better than others, don'tcha know, and I just wanted to be, just once, one of the ones who had it better."

"We've all had that feeling," I say, thinking about my cool apartment and how I won't be there six more months. "There are probably people who think you have it good. A farm, two houses, a good marriage, eight healthy kids . . ."

"You don't understand. I love Barb and I love my kids, and I woulda been happy if we had twenty of them. Or five. It's just the way things all stopped like that. Somebody always screws it up for me. That doctor screwed it up. Wasn't an act of God or the weather or even just bad luck. She just plain thought Barb and me had too many children, so she stopped it. Like she's thinking, Okay, somebody oughta turn the hose on these two, stop them."

"Peter, you don't know she thought that. She didn't."

He jumps up and paces. "Yeah. My mother—see, my father died when I was pretty young. Ten. So my mom and I ran our ranch and we did pretty well. This wasn't farming, see, it was some cattle and just growing what they needed, and it wasn't a big spread. Okay, so I missed my old man but still, he left me with something I coulda done for the rest of my life and been happy. Only then, my mother marries this guy, and his idea is, instead of paying taxes on all this land, we should sell it to a developer. So he did that. He fucking sold my inheritance, man! And then my mom, I couldn't see her much, on account of bad feelings between this guy and

edge here. Could have happened to anyone. I mean, I can relate. I've snapped. Yes even me, sane and sensible person that I am. I had too much, I snapped, and committed irrational acts. Dangerous acts. Acts that probably could have gotten me arrested but fortunately didn't. All the more fortunate since I was in my last year of law school at the time.

This is it, the thing I've never told anyone. I'd forgotten about it. Well, repressed it.

Oh, I had provocation. However, the provocation had occurred some months before. I don't even remember what incited me, the day I decided my upstairs neighbor was the unidentified (and unapprehended) guy who'd raped me, months before. Probably he looked at me funny that day, or something. Plus he'd borrowed my iron, months before—even before the rape—and he kept saying he'd bring it back, the creep, but he hadn't. Not even when I'd gone upstairs specifically to ask.

Anyway I was parking my car, and suddenly I went into a rage. I don't know what I was thinking; not clearly, for sure. I can't honestly remember anything else about that day. While parallel parking I spotted this upstairs neighbor returning from the duplex next door and *immediately* decided he was the rapist and he was gonna pay. First I slammed my poor little Triumph Spitfire convertible into the car behind me, both for spite and to get some maneuvering room. And maybe as a warning to him. He stood there, with his T-shirt thrown over one shoulder and an odd look on his face. Then I caused the car to jump the curb and went tearing down the sidewalk after him. Blind scalding fury. First he backed off, waving his hands in front of him.

probably should have at some point. In fact I try never to think of it. But it's there, along with certain other lapses and losses of temper, and for that, I should be able to understand a mind like Peter's. Going over the edge. Just getting completely fed up.

Except I flare. Unlike Peter Lookabaugh, I'm not capable of sustained rage. By now, in that kind of mood, I would already have shot the place up, done whatever damage I was capable of, and I'd be sitting in a bar somewhere, wondering if the law was on my tail. But I guess I understand it: blind, red rage, that instead of washing away, just builds.

And what if someone with some sense had tried to stop me when I went on my little rampage? I don't know. Somehow I don't think it would have worked. I might have stopped, but the rage would have been there, simmering inside me, and it would have come out again. I had to run through this on my own and come to my own conclusions, and as a basically reasonable person, I applied some kind of psychological brake. So maybe Lookabaugh needs to run through this himself and will put on his own brake.

Then again, maybe he won't. The papers are full of stories of people who run amok and kill other people.

Not that I'm trying to excuse myself, but my own little rampage didn't cause any harm, ultimately. Oh, sure—technically it was vehicular assault. But I didn't, for instance, shoot out windows, smash expensive hospital equipment, or hold hostages. I was satisfied with only minor damage, although I think I needed to inflict *some*.

And also, I was not cornered.

It might be good for Lookabaugh to get this out, but

I wish Alexi hadn't gotten into this. I don't know why I thought letting Peter talk would turn him into a lamb that I could lead out of here. But I know it's impossible with Alexi in a confrontational mode.

"You grew up rich, sounds like. Well I and most of the people in the world have to fight and scratch for everything, so you're no better than the rest of us and no more entitled. So, you lost your land in Aspen. Big deal. Most of the people in the world would thank their lucky to stars to have six acres anywhere, even Weld County! You lose some acres, you should talk to my people, they lost a whole fucking country."

I'm frazzled, desperate, and exhausted. Maybe because I'm so tired, I can see the dynamics change. The above-referenced reasonable person might think this conversation could lead Alexi and Peter onto common ground, but Peter is not an RP, and neither is Alexi, and neither am I.

I close my eyes, just for a second. Then I snap them open. I am no great shakes in the physical-fitness department, and Alexi is a pitiful excuse for a man— maybe six feet and probably weighs about one-ten, with really bad posture. But maybe working together, we could take Lookabaugh. Particularly if Lookabaugh's feeling emotional.

I'm not totally without resources. My youngest brother took karate for years and I learned about as much of it as he did. And then I took a self-defense course, sponsored for nurses by my hospital, which taught me a little more karate along with a smattering of judo and just plain dirty street fighting. The main thing I remembered from that course was that when you punched somebody in the nose you used the ball of your

go if I did that, and would it go off? And could Alexi manage to come in after me, or will he turn into a puddle on the floor? Puddle, is my guess. But the most important thing is what happens with the gun.

"Don't even think about it, Miss Vicky." Lookabaugh's teeth gleam at me for a second, then he points the gun at the TV and pulls the trigger.

cals and fumes and you've probably poisoned all of us,"
I yell. This is probably not the best way to turn the situation (and hopefully, the resolution) over to Lookabaugh.

"Noxious fumes," he muses. He's in the midst of
them. "Did you know that ten percent of all doctors are
serial killers?"

He can't be serious.

"I'm serious," he says. "Or maybe it's ten percent of
all serial killers are doctors."

I'm not going to argue. I use the curtain to try to fan
some of the smoke out of the room. Deanna coughs and
chokes. The baby cries. Alexi dropped down behind the
headboard of the bed when Lookabaugh aimed, and
he's still there. Maybe he fainted.

Outside, the sun is coming up, a fresh new dawn,
falsely promising a fresh start. We survived the night,
anyway.

"Okay, people," I say. "Who wants to be here?"
Nobody raises a hand. In fact they all stare at me bale-
fully. "Good, we all want to get out of here. How can we
do that? Peter? Are you willing to let us all walk away?"

For once I catch him by surprise, and I'm gratified to
see it.

"Yes? Good . . ."

"No," he says. "I mean, you're my, uh, my . . ."

"Collateral," I suggest.

"Yeah."

"For what? Do you think you can walk out of here
scot free?"

"Probably not, but—"

"You've made threats against the doctor. You've said
you want to shoot her. Then, you just implied she's a se-

maybe talk to her on the phone, if that would help you out. Help any of us out. Hell, maybe she'll volunteer to come in here and get shot. You think?"

Lookabaugh shuts his mouth and shakes his head.

"Okay. So that's out. What do we do? Get her on the phone? Can you think of anything she could say to you that would help?"

Lookabaugh considers that.

"You want to try talking to your wife again? She's pretty worried, I'll bet. Or maybe your kids? Think they've seen this on the news?"

That gets him, at least for a minute. He licks his lips and swallows.

"They watch the Saturday morning cartoons? Maybe they'll interrupt them with a news bulletin," I say, pressing hard. "How do we get out of this, Peter? You're in charge here. Right now, you can let us all go. We can all walk out of here."

"They'll shoot me."

Ah. He stills feels cornered. "I have an idea." I take two steps. I only pace when I can't smoke, and there isn't really enough room to pace in here now. My shoe crunches on broken glass.

"Here," I say, pulling a pink pad out of Deanna's provisions bag. "We can take this, wrap it up, put the little hat on it. You walk out of here carrying this, they'll think you have the baby, and they won't shoot." Part of my mind tells me this is a horrible idea, because Lookabaugh might really want to take the baby. And part of me thinks things might work out if he did take the baby. And part of me figures whoever's out there will shoot him, baby or not.

I roll up the pad and wrap a hospital receiving blan-

"I'm calling the doctor anyway." I pick up the phone. Somebody answers it right away.

"Hello, can we get Dr. Hawthorne, or some other doctor on the line? The patient's a little febrile."

Female voice. "It may take a few minutes. I think we can do that, yes. How are things?"

Oh, splendid. "Well, we're all here. Trying to find our way out of the maze, so to speak." I might be a little punchy.

"Hang in there. You're being very brave but don't try to be a hero. I repeat, no heroics. You're safer without them."

Damn, and I was *so* looking forward to smashing Lookabaugh's nose into the back of his head. Despite the fact that I have never been brave and I hate it when people call me that; it makes me feel like the Brave Little Toaster.

"Well that's the *problem*," I say. "We seem to be physically *safe* enough, but we'd all like to get the hell out of here."

"Can he hear you?" she asks.

"Why not?"

"Can he hear me?"

I look at Peter, who is worming his way toward me. Crawling so as not to expose himself to the window. "Doubt it."

"Okay. We may be looking at kind of a kamikaze situation here. You heard of suicide by cop?"

"Oh yeah. I agree. Get it over with." I don't believe that. After all, the man is fucking *slithering through broken glass* so as not to give anyone a shot through the window.

positive form, like, "Gee I hope I don't knock one of those barrels over," I would knock one of the barrels over. Once I nailed all three. It's like when you're learning hunter seat equitation and they tell you, "Throw your heart over the jump—the horse will follow." An old saw, but true, sort of. What they ought to say instead is: "Don't even imagine the possibility that the horse will balk at the jump, because if you do, *the horse will balk*."

Or, to take a more recent example, my sister-in-law needed to give her dog a pill. It occurred to her that this mutt will accept anything from a human hand— from broccoli to small rubber balls—and swallow it without half thinking about it or probably even tasting it. So she held out the pill. Something in her body language alerted him, and he wouldn't take it. So, she gave said pill to her almost-two-year-old and said, "See if the dog wants this." Since the innocent cherub had no emotional baggage, nothing invested in whether the dog accepted the pill, hence no revealing body language, this little trick worked. Only once, though.

Obviously Peter is smarter than a dog or a horse, and he hasn't turned off or tuned out the part of his brain that lets him read people. So, I need to think clean, positive thoughts. We *will* get out of here. Lookabaugh will not hurt anyone. Strike that: Lookabaugh is a nice person and means us no harm. Well, shit; that's not very positive, is it? It's like saying *I hope I don't* and then doing whatever you hope you don't; bad mental game. And on a certain level I realize this whole conceit is silly, in much the same way that, when I'm on an airliner taking off, it's silly to believe that the successful takeoff re-

The song comes to me in fragments. . . .

He barks at the mailman and he bounces off the walls . . . If he doesn't watch out he'll end up in the pound . . . He's tail-wagging happy to see you each night . . . You know he loves you, and you know he won't come back. . . .

Or is it, *you know he loves you, and you know you'll get him back?* I can't remember. Maybe it's both, in different choruses.

Lookabaugh hangs up the phone, looking profoundly dissatisfied.

I become an actress, playing the role of my life. Concerned for Lookabaugh. "They getting the doctor for you?"

"They want me to call back in twenty minutes," he says. We both look at the clock. Somehow it has gotten to be five minutes after five. The room is growing lighter by the moment.

"I think we should send in the squad," Chopak said. "Things are not getting any better in that room and the woman needs medical attention."

"One guy, four hostages, two guns," Swartz said. "Except, need I remind you, we aren't the ones who send in the squad."

"No, you don't need to remind me."

"I think we'll see what happens when he speaks to the doctor," Turlow said. "He's not threatening anybody. Hasn't shot anybody. In fact, seems concerned for their welfare. Just damned stubborn."

"Yeah," Swartz said. "But you heard what Vicky said, she's got a fever."

"A fever," Turlow said. "How bad could that be?"

"They pulled up something else on the guy," Swartz said. "Aggravated assault. Pending. That is to say, they don't have a disposition on it yet, even though it's almost a year old."

Robbins yawned. "That would be the complaint filed by the doctor, I believe. Barb—Mrs. Lookabaugh—mentioned that. And also that her husband got eighty-sixed from coaching her kid's baseball games, or even going to them. In the spring."

"So he's been accelerating," Chopak said.

Only Robbins was listening through the headphones now. "Baby's crying," she reported. "Think that'll stir him up?"

"He should be calling," Chopak said. "Oh, good," she added, as the burly hospital chaplain came through the door, accompanied by a woman in blood-spattered scrubs. "You must be the doctor. Just in time."

mean, you've got me all wrong. I don't care, people think that, think we were trying for a girl all that time. *Not true.* We'd take whatever we got. It was just that one we lost, that was a girl, and let me tell you it hit Barb pretty hard because of that, but it would have hit her anyway. And it costs a lot of money to go to China and get a baby."

"Costs a lot of money to have eight kids any way you look at it. They're all in private schools, right?"

"There's a family discount," he mutters. "Anyway, you don't get it. I don't want to go to China to get a baby! I just want what's rightfully mine!"

There's no answer to that. Or there probably is but I don't have it. Or I've already used it.

"That's a really quiet baby," he says after a minute. "I mean, a quiet cry. Really. Some of mine were quiet like that, at first, but the last two, David and Luke, they were always loud. And they all get louder."

It seems like a good idea to take the focus off the baby. "So, Peter, I was wondering. You said your mother died before you got out of high school and yet you weren't living with her. Where were you living?"

"I got sent down to live with my aunt," he says. "On account of I wasn't getting along well with my stepfather."

"Yeah, okay. A lot of boys, particularly that age, don't get along with stepfathers, or even their real fathers, and you know what I think?"

"Don't give me the Oedipal crap," Peter says. "I've had that. I may not have graduated high school but I know stuff like that."

"You didn't? I thought you met Barb in high school—"

I, too, was transplanted from my customary environment, that year. My father took a sabbatical and, for reasons I never understood, took us all to Norman, Oklahoma, so he could get a master's in history. My mother worked, for the only time I can remember, and she didn't like working, didn't like her job, and was a raving bitch the whole year, even worse than usual.

During the first couple of weeks of school we had to undergo what was called "Howdy Week," where I was supposed to say "Howdy" to all these strangers who hated me. During that week I was singled out by a bunch of boys—they could have been ninth-graders, but they also could have been seventh-graders, since everybody was bigger than me and I didn't know any of them. They surrounded me, kept pushing me into a chain-link fence, and made me sing the school fight song, which of course I didn't know, over and over again until I got it right. "From the hillsides to the prairies, comes a shout that never varies, loyalty that never wearies, We-est Junior High." I could sing it now.

"Yeah, I met Barb in seventh grade," Lookabaugh says. "That was my best year ever."

Mental double take: I thought he just said it was the worst. Now I *know* he's a psycho.

Reading me to perfection, he says, "The year before was the worst."

Even with Howdy Week and bitchy mom, my junior high experience wasn't a lot worse than anybody else's, although I didn't know that at the time. *Everybody* had a hard time that year, so bad that we couldn't even talk about how bad it had been until we were seniors. Or in college. Or out of college and in therapy.

but she didn't care about that. As long as they didn't mess with the words. And they never did."

Lookabaugh seems calmer. I focus my thoughts on the idea that he will give up. Peacefully. That he's a good person; that Barb tamed his wildness long ago and this is some kind of midlife breakout. A mistake.

"I'll bet you think she wrote that song about me," he says. "A lot of people think that." He sounds pretty satisfied. "But she wrote that about an actual dog she had, a long time ago. Before she even knew me. That dog had a bad end, but it wasn't because he was a bad dog. It was because some kids came down the road, shooting at road signs in the night, or maybe it was hunters, but anyway it was at night, and they shot that dog. You know the phrase 'shot down like a dog'? But really, dogs don't get shot that often."

He says this, of course, while playing with his gun, as if there's no connection in the world.

"But this one did. He had just enough juice to make it home to die. So, you see, he did come home. Come back. Not like the song."

I still think the song, at some level, is about Peter.

"I guess it's time to make that call," Lookabaugh says. I try to continue to think positive thoughts. Yes, he's calm. He's a normal person. Rational. Reasonable.

"You're going to call now?"

He nods.

"I think I'm gonna try to get Deanna up," I say. "Maybe walk around the bed. Into the bathroom."

"Good idea," he says. "She should have gotten up sooner. Helps the healing." Always the expert. But he doesn't pick up the phone.

about it. Except Lookabaugh who's probably laughing about it right now. Pleasant thoughts: okay. I imagine myself, some time in the future, back in my office, writing *Comp* on Alexi and Deanna's bill. The pleasant things are that I'm alive to be back in my office, and that it's not my money.

I rub my neck. Waiting: I hate it. I'm waiting for Lookabaugh to get on the phone and ask for whatever he's going to ask for, and then I'll check Deanna's bleeding and try to get her up. If she's been drinking her liquids, she should welcome a trip to the bathroom.

I turn my head to look at Peter. He stares at the phone with an absent look, the way he blanked out a couple of times before. Like he's sleeping with his eyes open. Well, the rest of us are ready to fall asleep at a moment's notice, why not him?

Without moving his head, he turns his gaze to me. "Okay, Miss Vicky," he says. "I'm gonna get that doctor up here now."

"And your people could just go in there and . . . whatever."

"What kinds of things did he ask you for, before?" Swartz asked the doctor.

"Things I couldn't give him," Hawthorne said. "Things done, that couldn't be undone. At first he seemed just normally upset. His wife stopped feeling movement. We expected she would go into labor on her own, but she didn't. We scheduled her for an induction, and that's when the problems started. He insisted that what we were contemplating was an abortion and that he had to fix it with the priest, so they fixed it with the priest. Then he insisted that we keep checking with ultrasound for a heartbeat, and we assured him we would do that. But that wasn't uncommon. That kind of denial—well, you expect it, in a late miscarriage. In fact technically, since it was at twenty weeks it was a stillbirth. But meanwhile his wife was very upset, because of course she knew the baby was dead, and any mother would be emotionally wrought up, knowing the baby she was carrying had died. And quite apart from the woman's emotional needs, there's a medical need, after a certain amount of time passes. You can't just be pregnant forever, although I've heard of unborn fetuses found essentially mummified, in very old women. In the medical literature. Very rare. At that point, both parents were quite understandably upset."

Swartz nodded.

"Now at the induction, which was essentially like a normal labor and delivery, the husband kept asking me to stop it. He was with his wife for a while but it was decided to sedate her, and at that point we requested he leave, also, even though we usually allow husbands in

past Barb Lookabaugh to pick the phone up. "Yeah," he growled, and then, "Tell them to stuff it."

"Hospital switchboard," he said when he came back out. "They're getting calls from the media, like tons of them." He looked for a moment at Harley, sleeping on the couch in the center of the room. "What did you guys do to the phones, anyway?"

"We rerouted just the ones in this room," Chopak said, indicating the reception area. "All these go straight to the fourth floor—it is the fourth floor, right?" Robbins nodded sleepily. "Any phone picked up, anywhere on that floor, will ring here and no place else. But we haven't done anything to the other phones."

"Yeah, we did," Robbins said. "Switched them so hospital calls that used to come in on that phone," she indicated one of the desks, "come in on his phone," meaning Harley's office.

"You know everything, don't you," Chopak said.

"I may be young, but I try," Robbins answered.

"Girls, girls," Turlow chided.

"Really," Hawthorne said. "I think I am going to go change and then check on my patients. I'll be back, if you think it would help. Personally, I don't much think it will."

"Yuh," Chopak said.

"Just so everybody understands that I'm not going to personally confront this guy," she added.

"We would never ask you to do that," Chopak said. "In fact, even if you volunteered, we wouldn't let you do that."

"Here's something else I found out," Robbins said. "The suspect bought that handgun recently. On June tenth, in fact. It's a Glock 26 nine-millimeter with a ten-

"You can pull that curtain," I tell Alexi. It's been open since Lookabaugh smashed the TV, and I'm surprised he hasn't had somebody close it. He's just been staying clear of it. Alexi shakes his head.

"Hello?" Lookabaugh says into the phone.

"Give the baby to Alexi," I tell Deanna. "We're gonna try to get you up. How do your legs feel?"

"Well, I can feel them, anyway."

"I thought I was gonna get to talk to the doctor," Lookabaugh says, and then, "Yeah, okay, I'll talk to you. Well, what I want is for the doctor to come up here. No, I don't want that anymore, but Miss Vicky says she's got a fever. . . ."

Alexi and I gently lift Deanna to a sitting position. She grimaces in pain but doesn't say anything until she swings her legs to the side of the bed, and even then, all she says is, "Uhn!" Then she hands the baby to Alexi.

"Just sit there a minute if you're dizzy," I say. I get her chart from the head of the bed—Deanna Dale Khosrov—and note that she was up as of 6:45 A.M. I can't check her temperature but I can do blood pressure. These typical hospital ministrations may not have any effect on Deanna but they reassure *me*. Blood pressure fine. I write it down, 110/80.

The chart tells me that what Deanna was getting through the epidural was bupivacaine and sufentanil, but since this isn't my realm, the dosages don't tell me when she might be recovered enough to walk. Arden very conscientiously recorded the time of birth, and the baby's Apgar scores. Good scores, 9 at one minute, 9 at five minutes, with "cyanotic" written in to explain why the scores were not perfect 10s. Cyanosis sounds terrible—blueness of the baby's extremities because of lack

"Um . . ." Alexi says. Either he wants me to leave, or he wants to leave himself.

"Want me to take the baby?" I ask. He shakes his head.

I try to pull my thoughts together. I close the door as far as I can and lower my voice. "There are people out there, cops, you know that. What we're supposed to do, what they advised me to do, is to sort of foster the idea that we're a unit, all cooperating to get Lookabaugh what he wants, all working together. It's supposed to make him less likely to kill us."

Deanna stares at me, wide-eyed. For some reason I choose that moment to remember the procedure was to measure her urine output. Oh well.

"I don't think he's going to kill us. We're just bargaining chips. Everything's going to be all right," I say.

Deanna puts her hand to her mouth.

"Feeling okay?" I ask her.

Her pained expression indicates otherwise, but she says, "Uh huh. Sure." Alexi is practically in the shower.

"Um," he says again.

I might not be the expert Lookabaugh is but Alexi's body language is written in bold-face capitals. "You need to use the facilities too? I can step out. But let's make sure Deanna can get up, okay?" Alexi nods.

We hoist her up again, then Alexi grudgingly hands me the baby. And I step out.

I don't know what it is about a newborn baby that makes us all think they're so beautiful. Objectively, they're strange looking. This one has the usual chubby cheeks. A low forehead. Eyes resolutely shut against the light. No discernable eyebrows or lashes. A few

ing to talk on the phone, just send her up." He slams the phone down.

"This might be the time," Turlow said in a low voice. "Two of the hostages are in the other room right now." Robbins nodded.

"The other room?" Swartz asked.

"The bathroom."

"Where's the baby?"

Chopak answered him indirectly. "No one hostage is considered to be any better or worse than any other hostage. And it's the parents who are in the bathroom, so the baby may well be there with them. Vicky's outside. Or so we think. With just one hostage in the room, I think we can count on her to keep her head down."

Swartz shook his head. "I'm not recommending that the squad go in shooting with a newborn baby in the room. We've come this far without a casualty."

"Those guys have been in place for hours," Chopak argued. "They could get twitchy. Why are they here, if not to go in? And this seems like an ideal time."

"They are *not* twitchy," Turlow said. "They're trained professionals. But you gotta admit, this is not their usual situation."

"Sounds like you're giving up," Robbins added.

"Hey, you know I'll stay on the phone with some-body for hours," Chopak said. "The best resolution is if the squad doesn't go in, in my opinion. But I can't even get the guy on the phone! Then, he doesn't call back! He doesn't have to remember a number. It's not like he forgot to write it down. All he has to do is pick up the phone!"

he could remember which of them was having a birthday when. He guessed it was a girl thing.

"What kind of priest are you?" Chopak asked Gifford.

"Not Catholic," he said. "Heads up. Here's the doc."

Cynthia Hawthorne came into the room, wearing clean scrubs.

"Hey, you had a call," Gifford said.

Cynthia moved her mouth into something that did not remotely resemble a smile. "I trust you took a message."

Turlow spoke to Chopak. "We gonna do this? Gonna call him back?"

Chopak's mouth set, no more a smile than Hawthorne's had been. "Yeah. We'll call him back. Dr. Hawthorne, you ready?"

Cynthia looked pale but steady. "This is a good time. I've got another one ready to pop before I get out of here."

"Okay. Don't apologize for calling him late. In fact, don't apologize for anything. And remember, he can't hurt you over the phone."

"Got it," she said, smiling a twisted smile. "Don't apologize, and don't explain. Ought to work out real well."

shoved into my back earlier, when we were walking around the floor. And I've been more convinced he really will use it. Still, I stand there, willing my legs to keep on holding me up, trying to shelter the baby as much as possible with my arms.

"See, if you're willing to shoot me to get your hands on him," I nearly slip and give the baby's correct sex, not that it matters, any more, "then you're not the kind of person who can be trusted with a baby." This sounds vaguely familiar to me, like I read it on a bumper sticker somewhere.

He juts his chin out. "What do you mean by that?"

I'm saved from answering by the phone. As it rings, I stare at it, mesmerized. In the concentric circles of my three levels of consciousness I not only hear but see the rings, the smooth black lines of the circles turning into zigzags against an electric green background. I stand there with the baby, and Peter crouches on the floor right next to the phone, staring at it, but neither one of us makes a move to answer it. For at least twenty rings.

Then it stops. The emptiness of it bangs against my eardrums and the circles smooth back like disturbed water becoming calm again. I may be going a little crazy here.

I am an idiot! I had the perfect opportunity there, to take the baby and walk out. I'm five steps from the door—and unlike Deanna I can move fast. After the first two steps I'll be out of Lookabaugh's range. Why, when the phone was ringing, did I not simply fling myself and the baby out the door? There are people out there—I know that. I don't even think they'd shoot me. All I'd have to do would be say, "Hey, the husband and wife are in the john, go get him."

"We'll wait a few minutes and try again," Turlow said.

"No," Chopak said. "Let him call us. Do it his way. If that's how he wants it."

"No way am I going to hang around here until that joker decides he's ready to talk to me," Hawthorne said. "I'm sorry, but I've been on call all night."

"But you're waiting for another baby to pop out, right?" Chopak said.

"There're other things I could be doing. Napping, for instance, or catching up on my charting. This creep has taken enough of my life."

"Is it true," Chopak asked, "that more babies are born at night than during the day? Or is that just a myth?"

"True," Hawthorne said. "The hours right around midnight and the hours just before dawn are particularly busy. Although people go into labor at all hours of the day."

"I always wondered," Chopak said.

"The myth is that more of them come around the time of the full moon," Hawthorne said. "Studies have been done. It's not true. They do, however, tend to cluster at the end of the month. I can't explain it, but that's been my experience."

"Interesting."

"And this, while not the full moon, is approximately the end of the month," Hawthorne said. "So I've had a very busy few days. Which is why I'm not wild about sitting around waiting for this nutcase to call."

"But he's got your patient," Chopak said, very softly.

"Which is why I *am* waiting around for this nutcase

At first it seems to be ringing somewhere in the beach house, where I assume someone else will answer it. Then I remember where I am.

This much is true: my neck *does* itch.

I don't know exactly how long this reverie lasted but it's easy enough to analyze, once I come out of it. Once I realize that I am, in fact, not in a beach house (I've *never* been in a beach house). I see myself as Rapunzel. I would let my hair out the window and help would climb up. The snipping off of this symbolic ladder symbolizes my utter uselessness in the current situation.

I scoot off the bed, squat, and pick the phone up— since Lookabaugh doesn't seem inclined to do it.

Then, since I have nothing to fear from the window— and anyway Alexi finally pulled the curtain closed again—I stand up, nearly fainting. And then I realize I need to say *Hello*.

"Hello?"

"Vicky?" Cynthia Hawthorne's voice.

"Oh . . . hi." If I sound stupid it's because I'm stupefied. Then it clicks. "Dr. Hawthorne," I say. I look down at her patient, who, if not sleeping, is doing a very good imitation of it, much better than mine. At least she's lying down, curled in a semi-fetal position around the baby with her eyes closed. Alexi, looking woozy, guards the baby from the other side.

"You need to talk to Peter."

"Yeah," Cindy says. "I'm really looking forward to that."

I cover the receiver with my hand. "Dr. Hawthorne. For you." He sighs as if this is a tremendous imposition and reaches up. I put the receiver in his hand.

"Well, hello there," he says in his hearty down-home

think this is all my fault." She wanted to throw the phone down and leave the room. The premises. She had already gone much, much further than she wanted with this. She liked Barb. Felt sorry for Barb. She couldn't get an image of the patient who was being held hostage, but she didn't blame Barb for that.

"I don't believe that," Peter said. "I believe you've been talking to her all along, convincing her to leave me. All this trouble started with that surgery."

She didn't need Chopak's hand telling her to hesitate. She had nothing more to say to him about the surgery. After a moment, she thought of something to say. "Mr. Lookabaugh, I'm sorry there's trouble between you and your wife." She wasn't. She thought Barb, or anybody married to this nut, should get far away from him. "But this is something you and your wife need to work out. I'm not part of it."

On the board, Chopak wrote: TRUE. MRS. L HAS FILED FOR DIVORCE. SHE DIDN'T LIKE TO ADMIT IT.

There was a long silence on the phone. Cindy finally broke it. "Look, um—I don't know what you want from me."

Chopak nodded, then nudged Robbins aside and wrote something on the board. MAYBE CAN WORK THINGS OUT AND AVOID SERIOUS CONSEQUENCES IF YOU'RE WILLING TO GIVE UP HOSTAGES.

Cindy saw what she was supposed to say. Or, she guessed, the direction she was supposed to go. What she needed here was Barb telling him that she would forgive him and would always be true, if only he'd let those people out of the hospital room.

"I know you want to avoid serious consequences,"

she acted against him. Grew less affectionate. Tried to come between him and his sons.

And then, despite trying very hard not to, I zone out again, although not as far out. Pieces of Peter's conversation drift to me and they are all familiar. Of course they are; we've been over this many times, and there's nothing new. Well only the one thing, that Barb is going to divorce him.

I wonder if she just decided that tonight. Then I overhear Peter saying something to the effect that he found papers, work sheets, that he suspected Cindy of sending to Barb. Hell yes, he believes it.

"Mr. Lookabaugh," Cindy said. "I am a doctor, not a lawyer. Not any kind of advocate. Just a doctor."

"A butcher," he said.

She shook her head and waited until Chopak signaled her.

"I don't send people child support work sheets and financial work sheets. Lawyers do that. Not doctors."

"You think I'm stupid?" he asked. "I'm not that stupid. I know there are people you report to. I saw that woman in your office who was doing some court thing."

Cindy realized what he meant. "If I see evidence of spousal abuse, domestic abuse, I have to report that," she said. "As I recall, I made no such report about your case. If somebody did—"

"You're saying I beat Barb up? I never did!"

Cindy gave Chopak an alarmed see-how-he-is look. "Mr. Lookabaugh, do you think I'm stupid?" Chopak shook her head and waved her hands, but Cindy plowed on. "You know and I know that I never spoke

wife consented to the treatment? Yes, she had. Had they cleared the problem, induction of a necrotic fetus, with their priest so that there was no conflict with their religious beliefs and the medical necessity of the procedure? Yes, they had. And so on, down to the part where both Lookabaughs admitted that the wife had made a complete recovery from the surgery. We'd gotten Peter that far before, only to have him balk. But that day, he hadn't balked. He had simply signed the agreement. I credited my excellent ability to isolate issues.

Well no, he hadn't simply signed it. He first read it intently, at times with his tongue sticking out from between his lips. He asked a couple of questions. There were items in the agreement I would have been willing to change, but I didn't have to, because in the end, he whipped out his pen and *signed that sucker*, all three copies, then went back and initialed each page (there were only three). Then Barb signed them. Peter also signed a pleading withdrawing his nuisance lawsuit. My assistant came in and notarized all the signatures, and Peter and Barb Lookabaugh walked out without saying a word. I heard Barb start up as they left the office; she was saying they ought to stop at Mervyn's on the way home and get somebody a new shirt.

Maybe Peter hadn't found Gifford's presence comforting—although the agreement said he wasn't signing under duress, and if he felt pressured, he'd had almost ten months to tell somebody about it.

I hear Peter saying something into the phone about avoiding serious consequences. Hah, no way. But of course they can tell him anything they want. Then he holds the phone up to me again.

"They want to hear from all the hostages. Make sure

"I'd hate to be held to any one time," he says. I look at the clock. It's after nine—which is amazing. I haven't even been here twelve hours. It seems like weeks.

"I have a couple of questions," he says. "Answer yes or no and don't say anything more. These questions concern the demeanor of the suspect."

"Okay. Hit me." I can almost feel him wince on the phone.

"Right. Now here's the thing, I want to assure you that everything Mr. Lookabaugh is asking for is appropriate. That is to say, he's asked to see his children, and we've told him they're on the way. Which is true. Of course, he will only be able to talk to them by phone."

I wait for the yes-or-no question. It doesn't come. Finally I respond. "Okay."

"Can you see him?"

"Yes." Now there was an easy one.

"Are his eyes open?"

"Yes." And so are mine. Barely.

"Are the pupils dilated?"

I hesitate and stare down at Lookabaugh. "Somewhat." As I say it I realize it wasn't a yes-or-no answer. But Swartz doesn't care.

"Does he seem lethargic or energized?"

"Uh . . ."

"You're right, let me rephrase that. Does he seem energized?"

"No."

"Lethargic?"

"No."

"Depressed?"

"Yes." Darn it, I wish he'd given me a range. Like

Arden must have mentioned it, and if she thought it was worth mentioning, I'm willing to give it a try.

"Only, I cannot overemphasize this, *only* if it doesn't jeopardize your safety or that of anyone else in the room. Or in other words, don't be a hero. But if you have the opportunity, it's a possibility. I feel it's only fair to give you this information. We'd really prefer you not use it."

"Is that it?"

"That's it." I hang up, turning this possibility, as he called it, around in my mind. "You can call them anytime," I tell Peter, somewhat distractedly. My words sound mindless in my ears.

I lean back against Deanna's bed again. Slide my left hand in the general direction of her pillow. I can't do anything; he's looking at me. Can't slip it into my pocket; my dress doesn't have one. (Evening clothes usually don't. Design flaw.)

Then I stand up. I'm not going to sit here and go to sleep. *Peter* can, if he wants. I'll even help him, if I get a chance. But meanwhile, I have to do something.

"I'm going over there to that closet," I tell him. "Sometimes they keep brooms and stuff in there." And sometimes extra scrubs. With pockets.

Lookabaugh nods. "Good idea." Then he stands up, stretches, and begins pacing. I guess he's falling asleep too.

reason I was magic when it came to starting IVs. I was a real whiz at giving shots. People said I made them absolutely painless. And in the OR, I worked better with the doctors than a lot of people. Of course, by the time I got to OR work, I was already in law school, which might have had some effect on the doctors I worked with.

And unlike some of the nurses who were prima donnas about it, I didn't mind cleaning up after people. Wasn't wild about diarrhea—nobody is—but I was never much bothered by blood, pus, or vomit. Remove it from the patient's presence, scrub it away—all that made me feel like I was accomplishing something.

Peter Lookabaugh doesn't help me. He paces. He opens the cabinets. Although he also moves quietly, and he doesn't slam the cabinets shut. I have no idea what he's looking for. I have moments when I'm desperately afraid that something in my body language will send him to the pillows under Deanna. I almost wish I didn't know what was there.

Then I tell myself that I don't know it's there. That helps. Somewhat.

My housekeeping measures convince me, briefly, that I'm doing all I can, although I continue to rage at myself for the lost opportunity. Hopefully not out loud. I also keep trying to summon up images of my life and in some weird way, the fact that I cannot seem to get any of my life to pass before my eyes reassures me that my time has not yet come.

Alexi kneels on the floor (the part of it that's been, ha-ha, swept), leans his torso on the bed, and stares dull-eyed at me as I clean. But he doesn't sleep. I have to give him that: he stands guard over his wife and his new

"When are they gonna call?" He sounds almost whiny.

"You could call them. Remember?"

He looks over his shoulder as if there might be somebody behind him, then back at me. "You call them. See what they're doing."

"You asked for your kids. I assume they've sent someone to get them."

"I thought Barb's mom . . ." he breaks off and turns quickly to the busted TV set, as if he's going to break it again. "It doesn't take that long."

"So call them."

Deanna makes a noise. I look at her; she's making a face. She must have heard us and realized where she is.

"You call them," Lookabaugh says.

I move to the phone, pick it up, set it once again on the bedside table, which is now four or five feet from the bed. As I lean on it, it rolls even farther from the bed, almost causing me to lose my balance. If I were watching me, I'd laugh.

This is awful. I really had high hopes for that conversation between Peter and Cindy Hawthorne. He wanted to talk to the doctor, he got to talk to her, and here we still are.

I sigh. What I need here is a surge of adrenaline. It's gotten very hard to care about anything. I pick up the receiver. I hold my finger over the push-button dial. Before I can even collect myself to push a number, any number, somebody picks up. The guy with the toadlike voice.

"Mr. Lookabaugh?" he says.

"No . . . this is Vicky." I straighten up. "We were wondering . . . what's going on."

feel if my father had ever done anything like this. I'd have been pissed off like you wouldn't believe. I almost didn't forgive him for dragging me to Oklahoma.

I turn away from Peter and to Deanna, who's running fingers through her tangled hair and trying to round up enough strands to make a ponytail. I formulate another wild plan—I'll suggest she take a shower, with Alexi helping. Then I'll cut out with the baby, while Lookabaugh's still on the phone talking to his kids; surely he wouldn't shoot us while talking to his kids. I quickly abandon this plan. They've got hostage negotiators who know what they're doing.

Judging by the tone of his voice, Lookabaugh is now speaking to the younger children. After all this, I'm sort of amazed that his voice does the same thing anybody's does when talking to a young child. A lilt, different diction. Although I don't like what he's saying at all—he's talking about the little sister who went to heaven. And having a pretty hard time explaining it too.

The mother-in-law, the mother-in-law, get her on there. It's like a mantra in my head.

And, eventually, he does. For me, it's a disappointment. I notice an immediate change in his affect: more respectful, less relaxed. But the conversation doesn't have the effect on him that his earlier one did. From my perspective the ideal result would be for him to say, "Okay, I'll get out of here. Everybody's free to go." He doesn't say that.

In fact it's a bitter disappointment. But at least he's biting his lip and agreeing to something. Yes or no answers, the kind I was giving.

After a moment he hands the phone to me.

I say hello, maybe somewhat belligerently.

the air. I have no idea what the negotiators promised him—or threatened him with.

"So," I say to Peter. "Are we ready?" He nods again. Into the phone I say, "Just a minute."

Deanna and Alexi have been following this with some interest. They're ready. Deanna hands the baby to Alexi, who grips the child in one arm and puts the other around Deanna. I help her up.

"We're going all together," Lookabaugh says. "You two first, then me and Vicky. You two go open the door."

With glances at each other, they head for the door, Deanna shuffling and still slightly bent over. Lookabaugh grabs me around the waist. "You stay close to me," he says.

"Right." As if I have a choice.

Lookabaugh nods at the phone. I pick the receiver up—although I probably didn't need to. "We're ready."

"Great," Swartz says and then, with an inflection that's probably supposed to make me feel good, "and so are we."

We step as a group outside the door. Peter looks one way, down the dark hall, then the other. I wish we could see the lobby, but it's around the curve. Way around, even farther than the kitchen.

Alexi goes first, carrying the baby, with Deanna a little behind him and to his left. Lookabaugh follows closely, protected by his human shield. Me.

If I'd worn different shoes, Lookabaugh would be at least five inches taller and he wouldn't be able to do this. But I didn't think to kick them off. Therefore, I am perfect. Not that it matters, since Deanna and Alexi are in front of us.

tors before I even realize what's happening. I wonder if he singed my dress.

"Oh my God," Deanna says, leaning heavily on Alexi. His arm tightens around her. I concentrate on keeping a tight sphincter so as not to disgrace myself. Clinically, I know why everything in your bowels (not much, in my case) turns into liquid at times like this. It's part of the fight-or-flight reflex. If you opt for flight at least you won't have a full bowel to slow you down. In the upper part of your gastrointestinal system undigested food turns into something else: rocks and noxious vapors. I feel some of that too.

Lookabaugh waits a minute, during which my hearing returns and I smell gunpowder. A smell that, oddly enough, I like.

"That was dumb," I say. "What do you want them to do, call off this deal?"

"Let's keep moving," he says. "Tell me, if they brought Barb up, how come we didn't hear the elevators ding?"

I think about that as we move along. "Probably came up through the walkway," I say finally. "How did you get here?"

"Oh yeah," he says. "That's right. I came through the walkway too. Wait—stop!" We all stop. "I heard something."

I wonder how. My own hearing is still muted. "Probably your wife, in the lobby," I say, hoping to get him moving again.

"I don't think so. Nope . . . I think they're sneaking up behind us. Or through there." He indicates the area we'd just passed. "This is fishy."

one side and me on the other. He can't use the long gun—not without letting me go—but he has the smaller one up and pointed into the darkness. He takes a step back.

It throws me off balance. I lurch to the side. Lookabaugh pulls me upright against him. "Don't try anything!"

"I just fell off my shoes. But anyway, they said—"

"They said they wouldn't shoot me, but you don't get it, do you? They lied. My wife's not there. They lied."

"We didn't get close enough to see," I argue. *This close* to freedom. "She's there. They're waiting. Barb, your kids—"

"Shut up." Peter pulls me backward, inch by inch. "Alexi saw them. Then I did."

"I didn't see anybody," Alexi whines.

"Oh, they're out there." Peter keeps stepping backward, matching Alexi and Deanna's steps, dragging me along. "Just waiting for a shot at me."

"But that's why we're all in a clump," I say. "Even if they wanted to shoot you—and, you know, they probably do—they wouldn't fire at all of us."

"See that—there they are," he says, talking directly into my hair. His breath tickles my neck. He tightens his grip on the gun.

Then I think I see something, a faint glint of metal, maybe, just beyond the elevators. I try to yank up my elbow before he has a chance to fire, but it's hopeless. He's holding it too tightly. I feel the kick in my body as he shoots down the hall.

"Move!" he yells. "Back into the room."

I'm now breathless with fear. This is the moment;

Deanna. While I grope under her pillow for the hypo I say, "Listen, I'm really sorry." She ignores me and continues to sob. Just as well. She could have asked me what I was sorry for. Things too numerous to mention such as: that I ever set foot in this hospital, that I came back after getting the sandwiches, that I didn't bully Lookabaugh right out of the nursery when I first saw him, that I didn't flee with the baby when I had a chance. And that I've been too much of a wimp to try this before. I palm the syringe as best I can, then go for the phone.

I don't even have to dial. Swartz is still there. Nor do I have to go far to work myself into a towering rage.

"Thanks a lot, you bastard," I yell. "You lied to us! And now he's going to kill us all!"

somebody giving some kind of orders, or at least that's what it sounds like. Or maybe that's what I'm hoping. The baby starts crying.

"Mr. Lookabaugh?"

I snort.

"Ah, Vicky," he says, sounding relieved. "Okay, listen, you may have one more chance." He pauses, waiting for me to say something. "Can you hear me?"

"I'm listening." I'm listening, but the loudest thing in the room is the baby.

"Okay. Can he hear you?"

"Probably."

"Can he hear me?"

"Doubtful." I can barely hear him.

Lookabaugh leans against the wall, the long gun at his side. I don't know what he did with the little gun, but then, it's disappeared before. Unlike me, he has plenty of pockets. He's pulled a little notebook out of one of them and writes furiously; if he ends it all for himself after shooting the rest of us, he's going to leave more writing behind than anyone.

"First, try and relax," Swartz says.

Yeah. Right.

"Everybody okay in there?"

"We're just *dandy*." This guy is a nut. He's as crazy as Lookabaugh. The baby needs fluids that I don't think Deanna can provide, both of them need medical attention, and we've got less than five minutes before Lookabaugh commits some unspecified mayhem. Then I blow air through my sodden bangs. He has to ask that. It's some kind of code. "Yeah. We're okay."

"Remember, weapons have a finite supply of ammunition unless they're reloaded."

"Right. Anyway, a hostage taker is less likely to kill someone he's made an emotional connection with."

"Don't you think it's a little late for that?" Ten-eleven. After being at a dead stop for most of the night the second hand on the clock is now flying.

"I mean, the connection's already there. Go on, just try it—but don't hang up the phone. Just lay it down."

I take a deep breath. Touch heals; hugs heal, it's true. But a mechanical hug, a false one, would be no good. It has to be genuine. I have to make it real. *Can* I?

I tighten my hand around the syringe. Given Peter's ability to read body language, or minds, or whatever it is, I have no chance of even getting close to him. Even if I did, how much chance do I have of sticking him with the hypo? About as much likelihood as I have of hugging him: none. I shut my eyes, exhale, and step toward him.

He tenses. Stops writing.

I look him in the eye and try to decipher what I see there. Here is a guy who's had it rough. Okay. I know that. Had a lot taken away from him as a child, or thinks he did. On the other hand he seems like someone who's always gotten exactly what he wanted, and it didn't satisfy him and he just wanted more, and more. His eyes are that changeable color, sometimes gray, sometimes green, sometimes brown. Sometimes dark and sometimes light. Right now: Pupils so large I can't even see the color of the iris, so they look black. Deep pools, with nothing at the bottom.

And what does he see in mine? Red, probably, with green-tinted pieces of plastic stuck to them, Merry Christmas. Finished off with bulletproof black mascara.

I pull myself together. It means something, that his

door, but I don't want to lose eye contact with Peter. I stand a moment, frozen. How is it that Peter is so pale when his hair is so dark? Then I open my arms and hold them out, not even trying to hide the hypo in my right hand. "I forgive you."

Sometimes, the things that come out of my mouth just amaze me.

He seems to believe it, which means I must believe it myself. With a strangled sob he steps into my embrace and even, to my astonishment, hugs me back.

The long gun, leaning against the wall, falls over with a loud clatter.

Our embrace is strong and desperate. Behind his back, I'm holding a hypo full of Nubain that could maybe knock him out, but might not, and even if it did, it wouldn't do so instantly. Behind my back, he's holding the small gun. I can feel its metallic weight against my shoulder blade. For a minute I think I'm going to faint, then it comes back to me. Peter's smell, the fact that he still needs a breath mint. Yeah, me too.

My platform shoes make me tall enough to look over Peter's shoulder as I reach my left hand around to uncap the needle. Careful. I don't want to stick myself, and I don't want him to know what I'm doing.

I've never really thought about the mechanics of a hug before. I'd always thought that hugs were equal, assuming fairly equal size on the part of the huggers. But that's not the case. One person's arms are underneath and one person's arms are on top, and Peter's are on top. Makes sense. I hugged first. It's probably not bad, and I don't know how, or if, I could have avoided it. But the position complicates giving him a shot because I don't have freedom of movement.

maybe it burns as it goes in. Some drugs do. As quickly and smoothly as I stuck him, he turns me around and presses the gun to my head. "You two!" he barks at Alexi. "Stop right there, or I'll shoot her!"

Except for one second when I feel faint again, I don't feel any panic. I'm alert enough to realize this is an odd reaction.

"Keep going!" I tell them. "Get out!" Then I continue talking to Peter as if he didn't have the little gun pressed against my cheek. "The whole thing was a dumb-ass thing to do," I assure him. "But the reason you didn't bring it, maybe, was because whatever was in there, you didn't really want it, did you?" Uh-oh. In a minute I'm going to start clicking my heels together and chanting that there's no place like home.

He answers me in the same way. Calmly. "Maybe so. What the hell, anybody can screw up. Right?"

"Right." In a minute or two, the drug will kick in. Or not. I don't know whether this dose was supposed to be intravenous, subcutaneous, or intramuscular, and it matters. IV drugs usually work a lot faster, but some work faster IM or SQ. Most drugs given to women in labor work fast. I'd have preferred an opiate, not that I had a choice. Still, I figure if it can take the edge off labor, it could drop Peter Lookabaugh.

"Temporary lapses in judgment, that kind of thing," Peter says.

I don't like the direction this is going. I wasn't wild about the direction I was taking, either. But the important thing is to keep him talking.

Before I babble further about how this is the first day of the rest of our lives, the door opens and the SWAT team charges in.

shoot him. And I know damn well this has occurred to him. So, the hostage negotiators guessed wrong. It isn't suicide-by-cop. Peter Lookabaugh doesn't want to die, either.

I guess that means we're all just going to stand here until somebody flinches. I chance a deep sigh. I want to say, just a minute, guys, don't shoot—any minute now he's going to fall over. I feel like I should do something, but the cold weight against my cheek convinces me there's nothing I can do.

And then it isn't there. And then Peter's pulling me down on top of him and I'm yelling, "Don't shoot, don't shoot!," and there's a moment of chaos during which one of the SWAT guys wrestles me off Lookabaugh and the rest pile on top of him. The one who picked me up shoulders past me. They surround Lookabaugh. I sink down onto the bed and almost cover my face with my hands, then realize I'm still holding the needle in one hand, the cap in the other. Very carefully, I slide the needle into the cap. Then I clench the syringe in my fist.

The SWAT boys are pulling Peter to his feet, frisking him, opening his jacket. Removing pens, pencils, the Swiss army knife, and various other things stashed in various pockets. Part of me wants them to do the TV cop thing—throw him face down on the floor, jump up and down on his back, and knock his head into the linoleum. The better part of me is appalled that I could think this.

"What's this?" one of the SWAT guys asks. He holds something toward another one. Like a pager. "Looks like a TV remote."

To me, it looks exactly like the Last Word.

looks cocky. Things fly through my brain: it's my fault he can't tell us where the bag is, but then, he wouldn't have anyway. I let go of his shirt and slap his face with all the force I can muster.

"Where is it?"

"Hey now," one of the SWAT guys says, but another one stops him. I guess they don't mind Lookabaugh getting beaten up as long as it's not *police* brutality.

"In the nursery? Where? You . . . *asshole*." I wish I could think of something better, but I can't, so I slap him again.

"Hell on wheels," he mutters.

Then I know.

"The isolettes in the hall!" I shout. "There are two of them, right outside the door!"

A SWAT guy stops me as two other SWAT members rush out into the hall. "We'll deal with it," says the guy who stopped me. "We've got some shields. . . ."

"There's only one out here," someone yells from the hall. The guy who pulled me back starts out and I follow him.

They've thrown something over the isolette. It looks like the kind of lead apron dentists put on you when you get your teeth x-rayed. The SWAT guy gives the isolette a mighty kick that sends it down the carpeted hallway, none too fast. And the hall is momentarily silent.

Before I can ask where the other one is I hear it. Squeak, squeak. Hell on wheels, for sure.

"That way," I yell, and take off down the hall. And just before the curve I see it. Deanna leaning on it, Alexi pushing it. They look back, probably in panic but it's too dark to see their faces. The SWAT guys follow me.

They catch up just as I reach Alexi and Deanna. "The

"Might be another blast. Crawl, slither, just get clear. Or there could be a fire. But stay low."

"Go, Alexi," Deanna says, between choking coughs. "But I just can't. I just can't."

The smoke sets off the sprinkler system, which drenches us, even before Alexi takes the baby out of the carrier. Hunching over her, holding her tight, he tries to outrun the smoke, and he's out of sight in seconds.

Deanna keeps saying, "I can't do it, I'm too tired. Swear to God I can't," just like she did when the baby was coming, and I tell her the same thing Arden said, which is that she doesn't have a choice.

There are usually wheelchairs in the walkway, if we can get there. I think I saw some on the way over. Ages ago.

Maybe Deanna remembers Lookabaugh holding the gun on her and ordering her to have that baby but she lets me hoist her to her feet and wrap her arm over my shoulder. Once we get going, she moves fast enough. Her increased speed, I realize soon enough, is due to the fact that one of the SWAT team members is on her other side.

There's less smoke in the reception area. It's easy to make out Alexi, standing next to another member of the SWAT team in front of the double doors to the walkway which, owing to the fire alert, have shut and locked. I leave Deanna's side and hit the button on the wall that will always open them. We stumble through, wet and coughing. Even the SWAT guys, with their masks, are choking. The doors close behind us.

In the walkway, it's like nothing has happened, except that instead of just the wheelchairs I remembered,

It takes me a minute to figure out he means the syringe. He waits, respectfully, until I hand it over. I guess he needs it so they can figure out how the drug might have affected their captive. Or maybe he thinks I might use it on him, or somebody. Probably I look like a desperate person. Maybe I look like a nut.

I make a conscious effort, as the guys in black escort me over to Admin., not to look like a nut.

He changes directions and starts asking me questions. He wants to know if I think Lookabaugh planned all this from the beginning. I do; I think he planned to blow up as much of the hospital as he could, whether he talked to Dr. Hawthorne or not. I think he just didn't get the chance to get back to his truck. Our security force did that much, anyway.

But I don't tell Swartz this. Since I don't have a gun pointed at me anymore, I don't feel it necessary to be polite, so I ask him how the hell he thinks I should know. He wants to know when Lookabaugh put the bag in the bottom part of the isolette. Same answer. He wants to know if I have any questions.

I do have some questions but I really want to leave. And every time I try to talk I have another coughing fit. Maybe I *don't* need a cigarette.

Swartz drones on, saying things that aren't of much interest. The guy who got blown into the wall by the blast refused admission to the hospital. Lookabaugh's injuries were caused by the blast throwing him forward and, since his hands were cuffed behind him, he broke his fall with his head. Good; they won't be blaming me for that.

Then I think of a question. "What happened to Lookabaugh's wife?"

Swartz doesn't have the answer to that one. He says he thinks they aren't going to hold her as an accomplice, then Harley breaks in. "She went outside. With her mother. They were going to give her a chance to speak to him. Peter."

Bet that was one hell of a conversation. "Were his kids there?"

Swartz knows that one. "His kids were never on the

"You probably should get some rest," Swartz says. "Of course, I'm not an expert, but going into another stressful situation—"

"Hey, it's not *my* wedding, I'm the maid of honor." And it's not exactly something I can reschedule.

"Incident reports, insurance investigators, patient complaints," Harley mutters. "You didn't even ask about the damage to the building, which could be considerable—"

I aim the invisible Last Word at him and flick the invisible button. Fuck you, Harley.

"The media wants a statement," Harley says. "Ruth's with them now but she's not sure what she can say—"

I turn to Harley—who apparently hasn't even been up very long. He still has brocade imprints on his face, from the love seat!

"Sleep well, Harley?" I don't bother to modulate the venom in my voice. Suddenly, it's all Harley's fault.

"All right," he says. "You know, you don't look so hot yourself. And there are people with cameras out there, wanting a statement. . . ."

"Fuck you, Harley." I press my invisible button again. There's my statement. *Eat shit. You're an asshole.* Even while part of me says calm down, he's on your side.

"Uh, Tuesday, then. Nice job limiting the exposure," he says. "Hey, what's with the thumb twitch? I really think you should just say something to the media—you can't get out without going past them. . . ."

"Sorry I called you an asshole," I say, forgetting that I didn't, the nonexistent Last Word did. "I've decided to downgrade it to simple jerk."

22

I do not fall over at Kate's wedding. In fact, her wedding is unmarred by anything anyone does or fails to do. It is lovely.

In fact everything has been lovely since I left the hospital. The limo picked me up, waited at my place while I changed, showered, and rinsed out my expensive silk dress preparatory to taking it to the dry cleaners for major rehab. I'm afraid the shoes are lost. They were fine until the sprinklers came on. Five-hundred-dollar shoes that I wore once.

The limo then deposited me at the spa, where I met up with the wedding party and entreated them not to mention, to me or anyone else, what I'd been through. They quickly agreed. Even Sassy.

I was soaked, scrubbed, plucked, polished, coddled, conditioned, and massaged. My hair, face, nails, and feet were primed and perfected. My makeup, applied under the direction of Kate's wedding consultant, looked as if it had been airbrushed on, and parts of it were. When I slipped into my Halston gown it even seemed I had lost a couple of pounds.

But I am not quite myself. I survey the wedding and reception from a different plane, as if I am elevated

257

No. I'm a visitor from another planet. Studying the customs.

I have enough presence of mind not to *say* that, of course. Instead, I just smile. I dance the Charleston with one of the more memorable men, a lively white-haired guy with a British accent. I dance the jitterbug with Kate's dad and fantasize about running away with him, taking a tour of the horse tracks of the world. I flirt briefly with Kate's one unattached brother.

The music doesn't sound like Kate at all. Where are the Beastie Boys tunes, the Neville Brothers, Guns 'N' Roses, Alanis? Guess those don't translate well to the local dance bands. Too bad. Maybe hearing "No Sleep Till Brooklyn" would bring me back to reality.

The band does, however, segue into a rather subdued version of Barb's song, *sans* lyrics. Reality check: am I hallucinating? It's not quite the same as the version played on the radio, and of course that one was a little different from the one Barb wrote, and I want to tell somebody but decide this is something best kept to myself, like the fact that I'm from another universe, in case I'm not really hearing it. I sit that one out.

Otherwise, I hold up great until the last song, "Stardust," when it finally occurs to me that I can leave. Go home. Brush the spray out of my hair, put on an old T-shirt and be alone in my place.

The idea gives me the heebie-jeebies.

The guy standing next to me—he introduced himself earlier but I forgot his name—throws his arm over my shoulder. "Are you okay?"

I look at him. Into extremely intelligent blue-gray eyes. Under normal circumstances I might actually like

BAD BLOOD

by Suzanne Proulx

Victoria Lucci's job as a risk manager for a Denver hospital is about to take an unlucky turn: Patients are winding up dead, and it looks like someone in the hospital is responsible. Four people have been given tainted blood. Vicki has suspects, leads, evidence, even the cops on her side. The trouble is, she can't help taking matters into her own hands...

Published by Fawcett Books.
Available in bookstores everywhere.

More hospital menace awaits in the
Adele Monsarrat, R.N., series
by Echo Heron:

PULSE

✢

PANIC

✢

PARADOX

✢

FATAL DIAGNOSIS